An Unusual Forensic Accountant

A Novel by:

Donald Macpherson

Copyright © 2023 — Donald Macpherson

All Rights Reserved.

No part of this publication may be reproduced, stored in a retrieval system, or transmitted, in any form or by any means, electronic, mechanical, photocopying, recording or otherwise, without the express written permission of the author.

Printed by **AMZ Publishing LLC**

1400 112th Ave SE,

Bellevue, WA, 98004

*Printed in the **United States of America***

I would like to dedicate this book to the memory of my mother who taught me the most valuable lesson of my life:

"Believe in yourself and always be positive"

Table Of Contents

Acknowledgments vi
About the Author vii

1. The Betrayal 1
2. The Infiltration 9
3. The Plan 25
4. Ghost Guns 58
5. Inshallah 100
6. Revolution 138
7. Retribution 159
8. A Change in Direction 171
9. The Conspiracy 199
10. Desert Hawk 217
11. M.V. Spartan 1V 232
12. The Mole 245
13. Islamic Students Association 262
14. The Showdown 297

(left blank intentionally)

ACKNOWLEDGMENTS

With thanks to my daughter Ailsa who encouraged and supported me.

ABOUT THE AUTHOR

I was born in Scotland, lived in Canada for twenty years, became a Canadian citizen and have dual nationality. I was a Captain in the Canadian Army Reserves and experienced life and work in different fields of Accountancy. This included being a Factory Cost Accountant, Financial Planning Manager for VW (Canada) Ltd, A Financial Advisor and establishing my own Financial Services Business. I was also a Sub-Postmaster and Assistant Manager of a Crofters and Farmers Association as well as establishing a Candle Manufacturing Business and having a Diploma in Hotel and Restaurant Management. I co-built eight houses with my wife, sold six and we operated two as a self-catering business. Lastly, I was also a chicken farmer (Sixty Hens).

DONALD MACPHERSON

AN UNUSUAL FORENSIC ACCOUNTANT

1.

THE BETRAYAL

He stood at the intersection for six changes of the traffic lights. Pedestrians anxious to cross the street were annoyed that he never moved and they had to manoeuvre around him. Some were quite vociferous shouting "Move It!" That didn't bother him, he was waiting for a particular vehicle and he wasn't going to move until it came along. He had picked this intersection because it was the main artery into the city after coming off the motorway and very busy with trucks and vans rushing to make their deliveries. It was a speedway with drivers racing their engines waiting for the lights to change, desperate to get into the city and get their deliveries over and done with. It was quite common to hear the screeching of tires as drivers burned rubber to be the first across. It was not uncommon for cars to hit 40m.p.h. and more trying to be the first to get to the other side.

Still the man waited, then his patience was rewarded when the right vehicle came into sight and stopped in the lane closest to the pavement where he stood. The driver was young, one of the so-called white van men and sure enough he started revving his engine, looking around at his competition, challenging them to be the first across.

The man knew his waiting was over, his time had come, in more ways than one. The lights changed and the man waited until white van man was almost across then he stepped forward, turned to face the van, bowed his head and closed his eyes. Death was instantaneous. He was tossed several feet in the air and landed in the path of another boy racer and that just made sure there was no life left in the body.

The police had to prise white van man's fingers from the steering wheel and he spent the next five days in hospital recovering from the shock. It took him one day before he could talk. Of course, no charges were laid, there were plenty of witnesses to testify the pedestrian had just walked into the path of the van. Someone said it was a true death wish. That wasn't entirely correct, yes, he had wanted to kill himself but it wasn't a true death wish, he had engineered it. Two years ago, it was the furthest thought on his mind but life is a tricky thing to control, events happen, decisions are made and ordinarily everything goes according to plan but occasionally there are blips that can change everything. It's the ones that are Ill intentioned that cause the most harm.

Ian Wright was a successful computer programmer working for a small engineering company and he developed a program that saved the company tens of thousands of pounds in its manufacturing process. This was mentioned in all the trade magazines and it brought him to the attention of a large pharmaceutical company with manufacturing plants all over the world. They saw an opportunity to poach Ian Wright who they thought could save them far more than the tens of thousands he saved his current employer. They made him a very lucrative offer; one they knew his current employer could not match.

They tripled his salary, gave him a company car, all expenses paid, relocated him from what they considered a backwater town and gave him a company house, all expenses paid including a living allowance of £5,000 a month, plus a life insurance policy of £100 million. On occasion he would have to visit their factories across the world and would be allowed to take his wife with him also with all expenses paid.

It was a very attractive offer which they made sure was hard to turn down. He asked them to give him a day to talk it over with his wife. He was thirty-five and starting to think the world was his oyster. They both agreed it was too good an opportunity to turn down and the next day he walked into their offices and became their latest employee.

They bent over backwards to make sure that Ian and his wife were both happy and gradually eased him into work. It didn't take him long to identify areas that with a few changes in programming, the company could save a lot of money but the real breakthrough came in consultation with their cost engineer. He was able to develop a whole new manufacturing process using an updated computer program with targeted algorithms. That saved the company an incalculable amount of money and vindicated the hierarchy's unwritten policy to prey on and poach valuable assets from other companies.

Profits were greatly enhanced and that of course lead to a massive leap in their own year-end bonuses. Greed was the major factor in all their acquisitions, however there was a dark side to their deviousness. Once they had milked all they could from a new acquisition, excuses were used to drop them from the company. The usual one was a restructuring with the inevitable redundancies. There was never any remorse at the effect it had on people's lives. They thought they were invincible, do whatever they wanted and get away with it.

Ian's breakthrough was all done in the space of two years and shortly after he and his wife returned from a well-deserved holiday, he was told that the company was restructuring and downsizing their workforce. His was one of the jobs to go.

He couldn't believe it; his boss was never available to talk to him and the manager simply said it was a company decision and there was nothing he could do about it. He was given one month's notice.

Despondent was one of the words that could describe Ian's feelings and he went rapidly downhill. His wife could not jolt him out of his very deep depression and they couldn't make any plans for the future. The company didn't want to know him.

He reasoned there was only one thing he could do. The company insurance policy of £100 million. That would be a big hit on their finances and something they wouldn't be expecting. Rash to be sure, but in his current state of mind, the only thing he could think of doing to hurt the company. At least he would be able to leave his wife something.

On the day of his date with fate he left her a note telling her of his love and make the company pay for what they had done and to make sure she destroyed the note. He signed it, *Lots of Love and make them pay!* What the company didn't know was that she possessed an unusual set of skills.

The funeral was a sad affair, a handful of relatives, a few close friends and not one representative from the pharmaceutical company that employed him. As she placed a single red rose on his coffin, she made him a solemn promise to avenge the company's duplicity and destroy the pharmaceutical behemoth that believed it could do whatever it wanted with complete impunity.

"Not this time, you're not," she muttered.

She started out her life as a forensic accountant then went on to become an insolvency specialist. In that business she became well known and in great demand. A lot of companies owed their very existence to her expertise.

Her husband taught her how to hack into any computer and the dangers of using the dark web and that knowledge was just between the two of them. In short, she possessed an expertise that was in great demand but could equally be used to the detriment of any business. Right now, she was clear headed with one overriding objective – to bring down the people responsible for the death of her husband.

She had one other skill she never talked about, only her husband shared that knowledge. When she was in her late teens, she developed a duodenal ulcer and all the potions served up by the medical profession only gave her temporary relief. She was basically in constant pain. One day a friend suggested consulting a doctor who used an alternative therapy not reliant on drugs. It changed her life completely.

Her condition was not uncommon in those who were under a lot of stress and she had been studying hard for her degree in forensic accountancy. The doctor told her she had to release the tension in her body and develop a new mind-set to calm her inner self. The answer to achieving that was exercise, pure exercise. One thing led to another and once she got into a routine of exercise, her body naturally adapted to the release of endorphins by relieving pain, reducing stress and improving her sense of well-being.

"All well and good" she said, "Are you going to give me an exercise sheet to follow?"

"Oh, it's nothing like that." He smiled at her.

"I want you to take up karate."

"You've got to be joking" she replied, "I'm not really into the whole martial arts thing."

"Trust me, don't think of it as a martial art, which it is of course, and just think of it as an alternative form of exercise. I want you to enrol for one month and if you follow everything you're instructed to do, I would be disappointed if you didn't feel the benefit. In fact, I would be more than disappointed, I'd be amazed. I'm going to introduce you to a Sensei I know, and take the look of disbelief off your face, show the same dedication as you do for your studies, come back and see me after a month, and tell me how you feel then."

She smiled, shook her head, shook his hand and said she'd give it a try.

At the end of a month, she saw the doctor again, this time with a beaming smile, said she never thought in a world of Sundays it would work but she was now a dedicated student of martial arts.

That was fourteen years ago, she now had a black belt, was an instructor and her outlook on life whilst always confident now radiated with positivity.

There was never a reason to boast about her achievement, she was not that type of person, and she quietly kept it to herself. Only her husband knew.

The pharmaceutical company had reclaimed their house and reluctantly paid her the insurance policy of £100 million. On this occasion their enticement to employ her husband had backfired and she had to threaten them with court action. They had to cave in, it was a simple, straightforward life or death policy with no caveats. No one ever expected it to be paid after all it was just a game they played.

She was now homeless and decided to rent a fully furnished flat while she made her plans.

2.

THE INFILTRATION

First thing was to apply for a job at the pharmaceutical company using her maiden name, Irene Stone. There were never any cocktail parties or social events so she wasn't worried about being recognised. The initial bonhomie when Ian first joined was reserved for his boss and she doubted if he would recognise her especially as she was now going by her maiden name and there would be no instant identification comparing her to the name. She would also change her appearance with a dye job and different hair style. No one would recognise the old Irene Wright with all the changes she was planning.

Apart from the company, there were specific individuals who fawned on Ian and set him up with claps on the back and excessive congratulations on the excellent job he was doing. Promises made by management when he made the big breakthrough in a new manufacturing process. They were all over him then. She started making a list but first she had to get a job.

She looked at the available jobs and there was one in I.T. And another in the Accounts Department. Either would do as long as she had access to a computer. She decided to apply for both and if asked why, her story was that she had recently come to live in the area to be nearer to her mother who was quite poorly and she desperately needed a job.

The H.R. manager was curious about the two job applications but readily accepted Irene's explanation. There was a greater need for someone in the accounts Department so that is what she was hired for. Recommendations from previous employers was a breeze, she just made them up herself, besides the simple test she had to do for her competency was just that, simple. She was told to start in the morning. Next was completing her hit list. Conveniently there was a board listing all senior executives along with their pictures.

The first on the list was the I.T. manager, her husband's boss, Neil Strang.

Day one, a new job, a new determination. There was a staff of twenty, introductions were made, job functions explained and very quickly Irene could see that most staff just posted information and it was computer technology that amalgamated that information into different categories and analysed totals to send to the different departments in the company. Nothing new there. Most staff answered queries from the personnel using the information and occasionally there was a hiccup that had to be referred to the I.T. Department. That was the weak link and she concentrated her first line of attack in that direction.

It was easy to hack into the system and get Neil Strang's password, e-mail address and the code he used to authorize transactions. Whatever she did now was going to be in his name. Her first attack would bring his name to the attention of the company hierarchy.

One of the key functions of I.T. Security is protecting information from unauthorized access to company data. Irene was going to create an update to stay abreast of recent regulations to protect the company system only she would purposely misinterpret them and leave open a Chanel to purchasing history, all authorized by Neil Strang.

It didn't take her long to install the change then she just sat back and waited for events to unfold. It took a couple of hours but soon there was frenzied activity in the I.T. Room. She could see this from the Accounts section because the offices were all in glass partitions and the I. T. Dept was adjacent to Accounts.

The man himself was now in the office ranting and raving, red in the face and obviously denying any responsibility for the miscoding. People were busy on their computers, fingers flying over keyboards correcting entries in the network. Irene smiled to herself, if you think that was exciting…

In the next few days there was a lot of talk about the major mistake Neil Strang had made but it was apparently caught quickly and very little information escaped and it was basically only historical purchasing information that would be involved, Irene had set it up that way.

Now for the next stage. She familiarised herself with the layout of the offices by walking around and if questioned explained she was a new employee just checking everything out. There were several areas that were off limits. Special passes were needed for entrance to them. The manufacturing centre in particular and the highly sensitive experimental section where A.I. development was the company's latest exciting new project. The bosses were promoting the idea big time. Their theory that you could program a robot to not only function as a manufacturing tool but allow it to adjust itself as circumstances change excited them. Fewer personnel, lower maintenance all meant lower cost and increased profit.

Irene knew there was more to it than that. There was a downside to A.I. and she didn't know if the company was aware of the complexities of its use or just ignoring them. Artificial intelligence has many benefits but inevitably is reliant on information provided by humans. There is a lot of talk about algorithms as if they were part of some mysterious science fiction but basically, they are just instructions to be followed in calculations that tell a computer how to operate on its own. It's called the program. What is science fiction thought Irene is the development of a chip containing electrodes that can be transplanted into the brain that connects it with everyday electronic devices without touching them. She didn't know if some guinea pig had been talked into giving it a go however, offered enough money…

Where the dangers lie for a company is when an algorithm is made from incomplete data or flawed information that reflect historical inequalities. Human beings choose the data that algorithms use and also decide how the results of these algorithms will be applied so if a machine is hooked into other databases in the company, it can easily perpetuate biased, incomplete and incorrect information which is why most companies are reluctant to go to that next step. Irene decided to investigate what the pharmaceutical giant had done. That information could also be instrumental in bringing the company to its knees.

Neil Strang had to go and she was about to make life very difficult for him. One of the key functions of I.T. security is protecting company information by preventing unauthorized access to company data. This is particularly important in the pharmaceutical industry where development of new drugs is a cutthroat business. An effective new treatment could mean millions to a company's bottom line. Anti-virus software and computer protection programs are particularly heavy in this area and are constantly being monitored. Any leak or infiltration of company activity in this area could be disastrous. This is where Irene decided to ruin the head of I.T.

She hacked into the system using Neil Strang's password and found the company was developing a treatment for asthma using gene therapy. From the looks of it they were pretty well advanced in finalizing a treatment and she knew that rival companies would love to get their hands on that information.

The best way to stitch him up was to provide evidence that he had actively conspired with a rival company to pass on information and you do that by making sure a trail leads to a transfer of money. She picked another large pharmaceutical company and hacked into their banking system. The money transferred had to be justified and reflect the value of the information received. Now she had to decide how much that would be. For a treatment at such an advanced stage it had to appear worthwhile for a company to pay. She decided a quarter of a million pounds would be an appropriate amount. Gaining access to Neil Strang's banking details wasn't a problem and when she pushed the button to transfer the money, she smiled to herself, stage one, almost complete.

Next, she had to open up a channel to the company's highly secretive website. Even though it was well protected with the most up to date anti-virus software it was a doddle for Irene to bypass all the controls and open it up so anyone phishing around would get the shock of their life. A dream come true; a veritable Pandora's Box laid bare for all to see.

It didn't take long for the proverbial shit to hit the fan. Word spread like wildfire and everyone was going frantic in the I. T. department. Neil Strang was there along with the Vice President and the Treasurer. He was trying to explain himself although by the looks and red faces on the senior management faces, he wasn't doing a very good job. Access to the company website was quickly shut down but not before a lot of damage had been done. That new drug for the treatment of asthma was now a write off... millions had been spent on it but with the information now available to everyone it was senseless for the company to carry on with it.

Irene could see the company security people flooding the area and start questioning staff. Neil Strang was escorted out of the Department arguing vociferously with his handlers who had a firm grip of his arms. The news very quickly reached the stock market and the company share price started plummeting.

This is much better than I thought Irene was saying to herself. It was big news headlines, featuring on the front pages of most newspapers. A senior executive at a large pharmaceutical company has been arrested for fraud. Neil Strang, the executive responsible for the I.T. Department has been charged with accepting £250,000 from a rival company for information on a drug they were developing for asthma and on a separate charge of leaving the company website open for infiltration.

Markets initially reacted adversely to the news then later on stabilised and the share price regained most of what had been lost.

The company was on the warpath. They were determined it would not happen again. All systems were being checked and a list of employees with electronic access to all areas of the company's infrastructure was being made. I. T. Security was on high alert, employees with access to systems were being interviewed and details recorded. What an absolute waste of time thought Irene. Management was becoming paranoid and that was leading employees to distrust one another and that lead to a company that was not very efficient anymore with everyone watching their backs and distrust everywhere.

In the Accounts Department, by its very nature, everyone had access to a computer. They all told their stories, honesty written all over their faces. Irene just stuck to what she had fabricated to get her the job, smiled sweetly when they were finished with their questions and left the office.

She had decided her next target was the manufacturing centre and its army of robots that were being programmed to work independently with the help of Artificial Intelligence. The company was so full of itself the executives had a gung-ho attitude and completely ignored all the warnings other companies had heeded.

As she approached the centre, security personnel turned her away but she was allowed to watch the robots attended by technicians in their white overalls and protective glasses from a platform adjacent to the control tower. It was far enough away so that no detail could be picked out, just an overall look of robots at work making whatever medication was on the list for today's manufacture.

As she looked at what was going on she realised that no one was looking at the technicians going about their business. Some of the women technicians were wearing hoods to keep their long hair tucked safely away and her plan was to get a pass which she should be able to do using a fictitious name so that if discovered or scrutinised would not lead back to her. Easy enough to get a white coat and glasses now she just had to look closely at the routine and work patterns. This is going to take a couple of trips she realised but she had to space her visits far apart so that no suspicions would be raised.

Back in Accounts the security people had left and everyone was talking about the new rules and regulations and comparing them to George Orwell's 1984. A lot of employees were unhappy with the changes and openly talking about finding another job. Irene joined in on the condemnation of the company's changes and the open distrust they had of their employees and actively encouraged them to start looking. The more turmoil the better.

A couple of days later she made another trip to the observation platform to watch the technicians at work. They still didn't talk to each other; they were busy looking at the instructions on their clipboards and making minor adjustments to the machines as they went along. Irene was interested in how the machines reacted to instructions from A.I. and today was one of the trials. She couldn't see anything different but knew the supply lines were being adjusted accordingly. I suppose it's all down to the programming she thought. Well, time for another algorithm.

She could hack into the computer alright but feeding instructions to the computer needed a password to point the finger of blame and with Neil Strang gone she had to get a new one. The Vice President is an ideal candidate she thought. He was one of the management cabal that heaped praise on her husband and then abandoned him once they got what they wanted.

There had to be more than one thing going on at the same time, attention shouldn't be concentrated on one event so she thought the best thing to do is bring attention to bear on the share price away from what was happening in the company. Share prices can fluctuate quite madly and all in the blink of an eye, somehow, she had to get activity in the stock markets moving again.

She started by making some anonymous phone calls to the news desks of several newspapers using a burner phone. The message was simple the pharmaceutical giant was hiding problems they had in their manufacturing line. The integration of A.I. was not going as planned. Irene reasoned anything to do with Artificial Intelligence was always of interest. After the calls she took out the SIM card as her husband had shown her and dispensed with the phone.

Feeling pleased with herself she went back to the Accounts Department and waited for something to happen. Something did happen but it was not what she expected. All hell broke loose. A siren went off throughout the building, security guards were rushing into Accounts and I.T. shouting,

"Shut down your computers and log out then get out of the building as fast as you can. There's a fire in one of the labs!"

The siren was loud and intermittent, a lot of shouting, women screaming although there wasn't any sign of fire, no smell of smoke, it was pandemonium. No one was paying any attention to Irene who seized the opportunity to get into the mainframe and leave a message on the company community newsletter. It was simple and stark..." Think of leaving, the company is in financial trouble!" There was no signature just a logo of the Scales of Justice. There was no way that message could be traced. Now she had to formulate one that could be traced back to the Vice President.

Too much attention, not enough cover work, the papers were starting to take an interest in the pharmaceutical company. The phone calls supposedly with secret insider information were gathering apace and taken seriously. The stock market was getting jittery and the share price was starting to wobble. It was starting to unfold just as Irene hoped. Some headlines were over the top created by reporters anxious to cash in on the current concerns with using A.I. Wild stories about machines out of control and left to their own devices were sending instructions to mix a formula using the wrong ingredients. It was all conjecture of course but Irene was about to make it happen using the V.P's password to authorise the instructions.

The security guards were making a final sweep shouting at everyone to stop working and get out. They stood their ground and weren't moving until everyone left. Irene had no choice. She logged off, closed down her terminal and made her way out of the building.

Harry Barnes was quite simply an arms merchant. He mostly supplied the criminal underworld but recently, new surveillance methods and the introduction of the latest X ray machines that could see right through large containers and detect the contents more and more of his merchandise was being intercepted. The demand was there he just had to find a different source.

He had a cousin who worked in an experimental lab in a large pharmaceutical company who came to him one day with a radical new approach to the manufacture of weapons. Cheap, easily made, light weight and non-detectable. Harry was sceptical but definitely interested and made arrangements to meet up and talk about it. They met at his home in a secluded area just north of the city.

"So, what are you working on now?"

"Can't tell you that but it's about the application of A.I. In a manufacturing process."

"Sounds pretty high tech."

"Oh, it is but all of that high tech wizardry has led to developments in other areas never imagined before. Have you ever heard of 3D Printers?"

"Can't say that I have, so what's that all about?"

"In simple terms it converts a virtual design into a physical object. Another way of putting it is that it is a manufacturing technology that converts a design into a three - dimensional solid object. The actual process is a bit complicated but now with the massive advances in computer programming all you need is a blueprint of what you want and with 3D technology you can reproduce almost anything, like this and he opened the canvas bag he arrived with and pulled out a semi-automatic pistol. It was made entirely out of plastic with a few metal components to allow it to withstand the pressure of a live round being fired. Other metal components like the barrel were bought from e-bay and local hardware shops."

Harry's eyes opened wide as he picked it up, "You made this?" he asked incredulously. "Does it work?"

His cousin produced half a dozen rounds of ammunition and said, "Try it out."

Harry eagerly slid the rounds into the weapon and went into his basement which was pretty well sound proof. His cousin followed him to explain how the gun worked.

A few minutes later Harry was all smiles as they went into the kitchen not wanting to let the gun out of his hands. He still couldn't believe it, "You made this," he kept on repeating, shaking his head, "You always were the bright one in the family."

The cousin said, "Okay, I'm giving you that one as a gift. You might want to show it to potential clients. I made that one on company equipment. Obviously, no one knows about it. Right now, there is a small staff so I could fit it in between shifts and dump the blueprint I used. They have a big industrial 3D printer that by the way, costs well over £2,000 and is able to comfortably reproduce the gun."

What I'm thinking Harry is that you manufacture the guns yourself. You're practically in the country, you must have at least two acres of garden and you can easily build a large shed, on it. Make it sound proof and no one will be any the wiser. You'll have the initial set up costs but after that it is peanuts to make whatever gun you want. You could take requests and charge up the kazoo for them. What you are holding in your hands probably cost around two hundred pounds. It is made of plastic so not traceable and if one of your clients is vain enough, he could have his own personal logo on it, you could charge him an awful lot extra for that service. I of course would help you get the necessary equipment, explain to you how to use it and you are in business...an instant millionaire.

"What do you think?"

"How big a shed would I need?"

Then they sat down to work out the cost and equipment needed and perhaps have five production lines going. They were getting carried away with it but Harry knew his clients and the potential was enormous. They agreed that Harry's cousin would make all the necessary procurements, set up the production lines, train Harry then he was finished. He would act as an adviser initially but after that Harry was on his own.

"Just one word of advice Harry, what you are going to do is illegal as you know but the N.C.A. are aware that small time crooks are trying to make their own weapons using cheap 3D printers, usually costing around £200. There hasn't been much success but they are aware it is going on so you have to be very careful. I know they monitor the sale of heavy equipment that can be used for illegal purposes but I'll be taking care of that, so just be mindful of what's going on in law enforcement. If caught you face a lengthy jail sentence. To counter that the rewards are exponential."

"Ok James, of course I'll keep all of that in mind, now I have to get plans in with the Council and get this shed built or perhaps there are some prefabricated ones available."

"I'm keen to get this moving as quickly as possible. What do you think, should I start off with one gun like this automatic, then branch out as I get the hang of it."

"That's the best plan right now, I've already got that blueprint and we can easily set it up on a computer. That's a major part of the equipment you'll need. We can make out a list right now so let's get started."

"So how many guns can I make in a week?"

"Well, if you plan on running five lines and do that round the clock, barring any disruptions with manufacturing problems you should average fifteen a week. I don't know how much you plan on charging but even at a thousand pounds each you're talking a lot of money."

"With experience we can streamline the operation and be able to make machine guns, then the world will be your oyster."

Harry just grinned.

3.

THE PLAN

The Vice President was in trouble. It had nothing to do with Irene that would come later. This was all of his own making. In short, he had too many fingers in the pie and it was starting to crash in on him. He had a highfalutin name that just exacerbated his pomposity making him the most disliked person in the company. Bartholomew Montague was privately educated, went to the best schools and spoke with a posh accent. That in itself put people off, it also didn't help that he liked to throw his weight around.

He travelled a lot on behalf of the company, arranging for the purchase of ingredients used in the production of their products. Invariably he was offered a cash payment, under the table, so to speak to gain his business. Quite often several companies were vying for the contract. They all knew they were competing and tried to outdo each other, offering increasingly lucrative incentives from expensive holidays to luxury cars. He was spoiled for choice and took advantage by offering half of what he would normally order just to get the cash payment then issue a new contract for the remainder and pocketing another tidy sum.

One of his dodgy contracts with a company he had never used before but offered more to secure the business and deposited it in a faraway country in a bank with his name as the account holder. Greed has a way of overriding all obstacles and it didn't seem to bother him that the ingredients they had used to manufacture their product were seriously substandard. Back at the factory, a lab technician mixing the formula to make one of the company's most effective medicines for arthritis was so used to the quality of the ingredients he got sloppy and didn't make all the required checks. It wasn't until the full production run of 100,000 bottles had been completed, boxed and on their way to distributors that a random check was made on the quality of the medicine. Immediately alarm bells were ringing and frantic calls were made to return every consignment to the factory. The quality control check revealed a product that if ingested would pose a serious health risk and in some patients with other illnesses, could even cause death.

The production manager was having conniptions. It had never happened on his shift before and he singled out the lab technician who had mixed the formula for his particular ire. The only thing that saved him from being sacked on the spot was the inferior quality of the main ingredient. On further investigation he discovered it had come from a supplier they had never used before and even worse it had been arranged by that blowhard Vice President Bartholomew Montague. Like everyone else the production manager couldn't stand the man and as soon as he arrived back from his latest jaunt, he was going to have him up before the Board. They hadn't received confirmation yet that the whole production run of 100k bottles had been returned and he was on tenterhooks waiting for confirmation. If even one bottle found its way into a consumer's hands it could spell disaster for the company.

By this time, he didn't think there was a single person in the company who didn't know what had happened. Suddenly there was a flurry of activity and the President's secretary was breathless as she delivered a message from the President, "Get to his office immediately."

Irene, like everyone else was absorbed in the crisis facing the company. It looked however that they had pulled it off and all the infected bottles were accounted for. It was time to take a closer look at Mr Bartholomew Montague. He was an only child from a wealthy family with feelings of grandeur that had migrated to his attitude on life and the desire to have all the trappings that wealth brought. His salary, while overinflated, was within the expected range of his position of V.P. in a high profit pharmaceutical company. She was able to hack into his private portfolio and his holdings certainly didn't reflect his monthly remuneration. That meant backhanders. This incident coincided with his recent purchasing trip on behalf of the company and she could see from the records he had used a company for the first time that supplied a main ingredient used in the manufacture of their successful arthritic medicine. That ingredient was now discovered to be substandard.

With her investigative knowledge and how to circumnavigate firewalls and other anti-virus software she discovered the company had transferred over half a million dollars U.S. into a bank account in the name of the Vice President in Santiago Chile. "Wow! She thought, got him, he's in deep doo doo now. I just have to get his password and make sure that what I do next will mean a long prison sentence for the erstwhile Bartholomew Montague."

It was easy enough getting his password, now how best to make sure his reputation lies in ruins and the authorities get involved. There were many scenarios going through her mind and how to perhaps get Interpol asking questions.

Rumours were everywhere so she thought she'd help them along by going the same route she had in the downfall of Neil Strang. Using a burner phone, she called the, *"News of the World"*, *"The Times"* and *"The Observer"*, in quick succession. An anonymous tip, a well-known pharmaceutical company had used substandard materials in the manufacture of a highly successful arthritic medicine that was now being recalled. She was on the phone for less than a minute and got rid of the SIM card and phone immediately after.

It was now breaking news and shares in the company, once again, were rapidly being traded and the activity in the stock market had the knock-on effect of decreasing their value. This was the second time in as many months that trouble had hit the company and questions were being raised about the management.

Irene was delighted with what was happening and was about to put the nail in the coffin of one Bartholomew Montague. The first thing she did was send a text to the President advising him to investigate the $500 K payment deposited in a bank account belonging to the V.P. In Santiago, Chile. The next thing she did was send a text to Interpol advising them a foreign National had deposited half a million dollars U.S. in a bank account in Santiago Chile and it was tied to an international pharmaceutical company trading with a dodgy manufacturer that had dealings with drug cartels. The last part she just made up so they would pay attention and perhaps work out a different scenario. She included names and details in her message, again destroying the SIM card and phone.

The last thing she did to hopefully seal his fate was transfer £100k from a rival pharmaceutical company into his private account with the message...- Thanks for your help. Again, it was no problem hacking into the rival firm's business account to arrange the transfer.

An almighty argument was taking place in the President's office. Shouting, swearing and screaming were the norm. Everyone could hear what was going on. The Production Manager was not holding back, as he put it, "I'm not taking any shit from anyone, especially you!"

The President kept on repeating, "But you're responsible, he's your lab technician!"

"Yes, I'm ultimately responsible, and the lab should have done the proper checks, but they didn't because they got sloppy and there had never been a problem before. That's what happened but it wasn't the real problem. The real problem is your halfwit, pompous and arrogant Vice President, Bartholomew Montague. He bought the ingredients from a company we have never dealt with before let alone heard of. He's the real culprit here. I'm going to report him to the Board when he returns from his latest jaunt."

They were interrupted by the President's secretary, "Sorry to interrupt but you have an urgent text message and two officers from Interpol want to see you."

"Interpol, what on earth do they want, did they give you any indication what it's about?"

"No, but they seemed kind of anxious and constantly moving around as though they had ants in their pants."

The President smiled at his secretary's description of the two Interpol officers but was inwardly quite worried. The only recent event that their appearance could possibly have anything to do with was the dodgy ingredients his Vice President had recently arranged to purchase.

How right he was.

The men from Interpol didn't mess about, straight out they told the President his pharmaceutical company was under investigation for money laundering and they were looking into the affairs of one Bartholomew Montague, his Vice President. They wanted him available for questioning immediately and he should have his lawyer present.

My God, what's happening thought the President and he explained that his V.P. was away on company business and wasn't expected back for another week. They looked at each other then told the President to get him back immediately and to call them when he returns. They were also bringing in a team of auditors, arriving any time along with a team from Inland Revenue. They also wanted office space arranged immediately. Their smart phones made a peculiar buzzing simultaneously and they both looked at the screens and the one who seemed to be in charge said, "That's the auditors here. Can we have space for them to set up their equipment? Thank you."

It was all rather bewildering and happening so fast the President's head was swimming. His secretary was urgently trying to get him to look at his messages, which she obviously had read. He saw the worried look on her face and looked at his messages. His face went pale when he read the anonymous message. The implications were horrendous. Throughout all of this his Production Manager was still present. The President decided, no use trying to hide anything and showed it to him.

"Shit! That evil bastard, He has to go to jail. It looks like he has brought all this undue attention, Interpol, Inland Revenue, Auditors. What else are they going to uncover."

Irene was on top of the developments and decided to piggyback Interpol's auditing. She just might be able to nudge them in a certain direction once she found what line they were taking and they would never be any the wiser.

Word had somehow got around that all the official activity taking place was because the V.P. had done something illegal. No one had any sympathy for him, just proving how much he was loathed. The Inland Revenue team were interviewing people they had singled out and had used the situation to their advantage by investigating issues they were interested in but had nothing to do with the V.P. And what he had or had not done.

Irene ignored their investigations and concentrated on the Interpol activities.

On the second day of the President ordering the immediate return of the V.P. he arrived at the office. There were no warm welcomes, he was ushered into the

President's office to be met by a hostile management and a team of law enforcement officers. His personal lawyer was not there.

He knew he was in trouble, sure he had taken backhanders, but doesn't everyone? All the other allegations were getting out of hand and where in hell was his lawyer.

Time to twist the knife a little deeper. Looking at the Vice President's two-million-pound mansion and checking how much of a mortgage he had she was not too surprised to find out that it was debt free. What a stupid man. Even if he had the money to pay for it, the prudent thing to do was to hold back, not draw attention to a mortgage free home when his income didn't support such a grandiose purchase. She also wouldn't be surprised that knowing his personality, he would have no compunction at boasting to all and sundry that it was free and clear of all encumbrances. Doing that would just further cement his fate. What a stupid, stupid man. It wouldn't take Inland Revenue long to put two and two together but she thought she would help them along.

She first went in to the Accounts Payable Ledger looking for payments to companies for ingredients the V.P. had arranged. From there she was able to hack into the supplier accounts looking for extraneous payments that could be linked to Bartholomew Montague. All these suppliers had slush funds for just such payments, some companies were cleverer than others at hiding them but Irene was able to make a list of payments some were for withdrawals of cash that coincided with the V.P.'s visit. She smiled to herself, Interpol and Inland Revenue are going to love this.

Another anonymous message was sent and she included a copy to the President. That should help seal his fate and Irene waited for the reaction. Because the offices were all divided with glass partitions Irene had a clear view of what was going on. It didn't take long. Handcuffs were produced and Bartholomew Montague was led away shouting and screaming his head off. The President's face was ashen.

A short time later it was announced that the V.P. had been arrested and charged with fraud and money laundering. Investigations into the company were now under intense scrutiny and auditors from both agencies were increasing their activities.

Irene smiled and said to herself, "Now who's next?"

The next one had to be from production. If she got her calculations right and used the right algorithm A.I. was going to take the initial blame but ultimately it was the person responsible for the production line that was going to take the hit. Irene didn't know who that was and didn't really care, her overriding mission was to destroy the company

She went down to the observation platform again and watched what the technicians were doing. One appeared to verify what the other was doing. There were six technicians and they appeared to be split into twos. It was quite intense and security guards were everywhere.

Back in the Accounts Dept she more or less worked on her own so what she did was not really scrutinized. She set to and called up the daily production schedule. As luck would have it the current medicine being prepared for production was being set up by a robot that had been programmed by A.I. It was perfect timing, she was just able to complicate the instructions, this time using the production manager's password. The instructions she relayed were for another medicine. Now this is going to be interesting. She wanted to watch how the robot coped with the conflicting instructions and went to her locker where she kept a wig, white lab coat and horn-rimmed glasses that were non-prescription. The identification tag she used had a fake name that she made up tongue in cheek, Alice Blowhard. She had placed it in the employee roster of the Laboratory Dept so that if checked it would be verified as kosher.

She got her disguise on and made her way to the observation platform. There were quite a few people there and she surmised it was to check how the A.I. programmed robot performed. Security was tight and she was asked twice for her identification. Suddenly it was all quiet, the buzz had gone and everyone was concentrating on the robots. The one everyone was interested in had a flurry of activity about it. Technicians were looking at clipboards, making adjustments to the line, in general, shaking their heads and Irene, while she couldn't hear it, could see a lot of swearing and shouting going on. There were a lot of red faces then the Production Manager threw his clipboard on the floor and gesticulated with his arms to stop everything.

Everyone started to leave then, talking amongst themselves, something had obviously gone wrong. Someone suggested the company wasn't experienced enough to apply A.I. to a manufacturing line. There seemed to be a lot of agreement in that.

Back in her office she wanted more detail of what had happened in the production line so she hacked into the President's email and messaging services to see the reaction.

First message to the Production Manager simply said, "What the hell went wrong?"

"Two sets of instructions were sent to the robot, both different, it got confused and started mixing all the wrong ingredients. It was all set to manufacture a product with a mixture of ingredients."

"Who sent different instructions?"

There was a moment's hesitation before the Production Manager replied. "The instructions were sent in my name.

Please note that I said they were sent in my name... I did not send them!"

"What do mean you did not send them? We set up a fool proof system that anyone sending instructions had their own secret password, known only to themselves."

"So, if you claim you did not send them, who did and why? Our system is fool proof. The only way for instructions to be sent is by using that password. Did you tell someone what it was, did you write it down someplace where someone could see it? Why would someone do that? Were the two medicines scheduled for production and you got the times mixed up?"

"No! The only explanation I can come up with is that someone hacked into the system and did this deliberately. If they did that only one of two things could be happening, either someone from outside, a competitor perhaps, trying to mess us up or we have a saboteur inside the company trying to destroy us."

"I have trouble believing that. We have the best I. T. technicians and they have designed a fool proof system no one can hack into our system without alarm bells going off. We would be aware of it immediately."

"Unfortunately, that's not quite true. There is always someone better than another and I am telling you, I did not do this!"

"Then the only thing I can do is get the I.T. department to conduct a minute investigation or perhaps get some exterior consultants in to investigate."

"That would be my recommendation because, and I repeat this, I had nothing to do with it!"

Irene took all this in and thought, I suppose it was only a matter of time. Time for a diversion.

The first thing she did was send off a message to the newspapers and the newsrooms of all the T. V. Networks alerting them to the potential dangers of using A.I. to control a production line and of the near disastrous production of life saving medicines by the pharmaceutical giant that had factories in other countries with dubious control systems that almost released a drug manufactured by a robot that got its ingredients mixed up.

She now decided to bring the President into focus and highlight his background and decision making in his previous career and what was now happening to the pharmaceutical company he was in charge of and perhaps introducing a few white lies or decisions he had made that could have different interpretations steering the company in a different direction.

Multiple attacks now, if the company was onto her and monitoring I.T. meetings and correspondence to do with hiring outside sources. Next, she wanted to find out when the company introduced Artificial Intelligence and how it had been used so far and who controlled its use.

One lab technician working in an experimental lab had the idea of using the fast-developing Artificial Intelligence to program robots used in a manufacturing line. That would take away the need for human involvement. Ingredients could then be fed into the production line, controlled by the robots and work twenty-four hours a day. Increased efficiency, increased, productivity and increased profitability. It was a no brainer.

James Barnes found himself in front of the management team explaining his ideas. Profit was the ultimate goal and it could be clearly seen that introducing a system that James was proposing would have a considerable effect on the Balance Sheet. He was given a separate lab and all the equipment he needed. His budget was high and it coincided with management's high expectations. Thing was, he had to deliver. He was given six months to prove himself.

Once all his equipment was set up, he started proving himself almost immediately. He bought the largest industrial 3D printer available and started manufacturing spare parts for machinery that had broken down. Gone were the days of sourcing parts and waiting weeks for delivery. All he needed was a blueprint and sometimes the addition of a metal part here and there. Smaller 3D printers were now the norm in most dental surgeries where it only took an hour or so to make a cap or a new tooth. He had several of these smaller printers that he used to keep a store of parts that were prone to breaking down so he was always on top of inventory. Management was delighted with the results and now the trial runs of using A.I. were over and the real thing was starting operations.

It should be working perfectly but someone had screwed it up. He doubted very much if the Production Manager had doubled up on the instructions fed to the robots. That just left it to someone infiltrating the system and purposefully feeding conflicting instructions to the robots. There was nothing wrong with the programmed instructions to the robot. He had checked and rechecked and gone over them with the Product Manager and the conclusion was, it was done on purpose. It did however highlight that programming had to be tightened to prevent the overriding of established instructions.

Irene had worked her way through the A.I. set up and now knew the history behind the pharmaceutical company's foray into this new field. To understand it better she followed the trail of parts and products used to make new parts. It was quite fascinating how science had progressed to the point of machines now determining, in this case, how medicines were manufactured. Quite frightening really but I suppose that's the way of the world, always moving forward.

She almost missed it, but her background had programmed her to a different mindset Why was so much attention being paid to the manufacture of one part, why so many trials, why so many different types of plastic. What was the part that required so much attention and trials to get it right? A lot of the information had been dumped but what people didn't understand was that even though the information was no longer visible on a computer, it left a trail and if you knew what you were doing that information could be reinstated. Irene had that ability.

When it all flashed up on the screen, she made a double take. Her eyes opened wide. It was a handgun! She realized she had stumbled into something very, very, serious.

My God she thought, what on earth is going on here. She knew about the use of 3D printers in dentistry, but manufacturing guns! She had a lot of thinking and research to do. Sometime later she realized there was a revolution going on. Workable hand guns could be printed on a home 3D printer. Manufacturing had to be of the highest quality and metal parts should be used to give the gun strength otherwise it was liable to blow up in your face when fired. Blueprints for all manner of weapons including machine guns were readily available on the internet. Metal 3D printers were also being used to manufacture parts along with industrial size machinery to make some of the metal parts ending up with an efficient, safe to use weapon. The staggering realization for Irene was that these weapons could be made at home. They were known as Ghost Guns because there was no way to trace them, they had no markings or serial numbers. Don't tell me this is a sideline for the pharmaceutical company she thought, or more than likely, a rogue employee. The finger of suspicion pointed in the direction of the lab technician James Barnes.

Her computer was flashing her an alert. The President had authorized the use of an external firm of computer specialists to investigate the supposed hacking of the company's computer system. This might change things she thought and she had to be prepared to make a hasty exit but before that eventuality she still had things to do that were much easier from inside rather than outside the company.

Let's see what this firm of computer specialists is like and whether she had something to worry about. This time she chose the Treasurer to mess with. He was responsible for the company's finances and ultimately approved all expenditures but he also had another very important function. The company was very profitable and it was his responsibility to invest excess cash to its benefit. It was really quite impressive how much the company had been able to set aside and the management of that money was carefully monitored and any investment had to be analysed very carefully and decisions made by a board of governors with one of them being from outside the company. That governor was changed periodically. He seemed a likely candidate for further attention.

No problem getting his name, no password was necessary because he didn't have one, didn't need one, he was the Vice President of the Bank the company used. Let's see if I can introduce a little bit of collusion she thought.

Daniel Smith was a long-time bank employee. After completing his business degree at university, he started work at the bank as a junior investment analyst, a job that he was in for three years before being transferred to a branch office for further training. He eventually became the manager and was in that position for five years before being transferred back to head office to be put in charge of new business. He worked hard and moved his way up the company to eventually become the youngest Vice President the bank had ever employed.

He shared an interest with one of the company governors, snorkelling and diving. They were both qualified scuba divers and both had dived in the Caribbean and the Mediterranean. Their shared experiences lead to frequent holidays together and with their families. They were both well paid but it was expensive hiring cottages, boats and scuba gear not to count the cost of actually getting to their destination. They also both had big mortgages so every now and then their lifestyle resulted in the use of their overdraft facilities.

They were out socializing with a friend one night and at the end of the evening their friend paid saying he had an expense account for entertaining and one of them could get the next one. It had actually never occurred to either one of them to use their expense accounts so they started doing just that, taking turnabout, only they got carried away with their extravagances and soon found themselves in deep financial problems.

Irene could see all of this from hacking into their personal accounts and thought it was the perfect storm. The bank vice president, the pharmaceutical governor and the treasurer all deserved each other so she helped them out by creating an account in an offshore company and called it the "Swinging Dicks". That name should draw attention to it immediately. All she had to do now was make it active by transferring some money into it and she thought, three dicks, three million pounds. The money had to come out of the pharmaceutical Investment Fund and using the Treasurer's password, with a simple touch on the keyboard, the deed was done. She wasn't finished with them yet, each one of them had to have actively transferred and used money from their offshore account in their personal bank accounts. She thought £150 K each would be ample, they were all active accounts so the money wouldn't be obvious right away but it sure would make a difference to their negative balances.

I wonder if any of them will fess up to the money transfer or confer with each other or perhaps think one of them had transferred money without telling the others. An interesting study in human nature she thought. Now she just had to wait and see what the "Swinging Dicks" did.

She had to be a bit more cautious now that they appeared to be concentrating on finding a "Saboteur" in the company so she decided to switch away from the head office and have a look at one of the subsidiaries. They had factories in Canada and France but the Canadian company was very involved in nano medicine that amongst other things delivered drugs to target a particular part of the body. It was a separate company that was leading the field in nanotechnology and had made several medical breakthroughs in that field so she decided to leave it alone and concentrate on bringing down the company that had destroyed her husband.

Back to the robots and the manufacturing line. She went to her locker, put on her disguise and went down to the observation room. This time there was a definite increase in security and she was asked four times for identification. That made her think she could only try her luck so many times and perhaps she should just stick to using her computer and keep a low profile. She was too late. Two security guards approached her and asked her to come into their office standing on either side to escort her.

"What is this all about?" Refusing to move an inch.

"We've noticed you down here several times and we just want to find out your interest in the manufacturing line, that's all."

"Everyone is interested in how the robots work, it's as simple as that. From what I can see everyone comes here all the time. Why would the company build this observation area if they didn't want employees to observe the robots in action?"

Maybe they were being super cautious or told to be on the lookout for excessive returns by employees, whatever it was they weren't going to budge and they took a firm grip of her arms and started to move towards their office.

She didn't struggle, didn't make a fuss, didn't draw attention to herself, just let herself be guided into their office. She waited until they closed the door and looked around. It wasn't a large office, there were no windows and it was down a corridor well away from the production line. What happened next depended entirely on them. There was one desk and two chairs. She was not invited to sit down, the guards had taken the chairs for themselves and looked at her rather insolently. She thought to herself, that alone was one strike against them.

She said nothing, just stood there with one leg slightly in front of the other, her body slightly to one side and her arms loosely by her side.

They started by repeating the question, why are you here, she replied, I've already answered that. She then looked at her watch and said, "I have to go back to work or I'll be late, if there's nothing else, I'll just leave."

She made a move to the door at which point both guards stood up and barred her exit. One growled, "You'll leave when we tell you."

She smiled sweetly at them and said, "I don't think so, you know you boys have a terrible attitude, if you don't allow me to leave, right now, I'm going to have you charged with wrongful detention, understand?"

She then made a move to open the door and was immediately and forcefully pushed away.

The guards had made the wrong decision. They never really knew what happened next, it was over in a blur. She was rougher than she could have been but she reckoned that they deserved more and she was restraining herself. As it was, both guards wound up with broken arms, broken jaws and they would be limping for a long time to come. They were unconscious for two hours.

Irene slipped out of the guard's room and slowly walked away using a different route. She went directly to her locker and put her entire disguise, lab coat, wig, glasses, the lot, into a carrier bag and walked down the stairs to the basement. The incinerator door was unlocked and as luck would have it, she was alone, so was able to open the incinerator and throw the carrier bag in.

She made sure no one saw her go back into her office and quietly started working on her computer again. It took about half an hour then sirens went off throughout the building. This was followed by security guards running around checking all the offices and every nook and cranny they could find. They used clipboards to register every person they came across and their location. The office workers were sent home and the security guards then started accounting for everyone else in the building. Irene went home to plan her next move and make preparations, if she had to make a swift retreat.

The next day the whole building was full of gossip about what had happened to the two security guards. It was generally accepted that they were particularly heavy handed and others voiced complaints about their aggressive behaviour. The mystery was, who had "Kicked the Shit "out of them and the general feeling was that they got what they deserved. No one seemed to relate the incident in any way to computer infiltration. Irene felt relieved, looks like she had got away with it, but she would have to be more aware from now on.

The auditors were back. These were not the computer specialists the president had hired to trace the so-called saboteur but the regular team of accountants the company hired to verify the annual accounts. Irene was surprised at the speed they arrived at company headquarters and hacked into the Presidents messages to find out what was happening. It transpired that a failsafe had been installed in the company's Investment Fund. All major transfers out of that fund had to have an approval number that could be traced to the governors who had approved it. All investments, once approved were run past the President who had no involvement in the investment process but had the final approval. This was the final safety check.

While Irene had successfully moved the three million pounds to the "Swinging Dicks" offshore account she didn't have that all important number assigned to major investments. That was one procedure she was not aware of. The transfer had been brought to the attention of the President and he was instantly aware of the breech in protocol. Mindful of the recent arrest of the V.P. for fraud and money laundering he knew something was amiss and immediately contacted the Company Auditors to investigate without delay.

They were very efficient, knowing about the V.P. and the charges against him. Nothing was going to be missed on this inspection. Clearly, there was some skullduggery afoot as the senior auditor put it, and the team was told to work around the clock if necessary to discover who had transferred the three million pounds and why wasn't it registered. It didn't take them long to discover it was the Treasurer who had transferred the money to an offshore account called, "The Swinging Dicks", and shortly after that the names of the three members.

The auditors made their report to the President without delay and to say rage was the instant reaction, would be an understatement. The auditors however had added a caveat. "These are the facts that we uncovered. As to their authenticity, that has yet to be verified."

When the President hauled the Treasurer into his office and confronted him with the auditor's findings, of course, he denied everything. The police were called to arrest the bank V.P. and the pharmaceutical governor, the third member of the "Swinging Dicks" was also arrested and cautioned. Everyone proclaimed their innocence. The President was having none of that. He interviewed each one separately, his Treasurer first. "Don't tell me you are not guilty; you've transferred £150 K into your personal bank account."

The Treasurer said, "Do you think I'd be that stupid to blatantly transfer three million pounds into an account with a name like that? and has any of that £150K been spent? and when you look at my account does it look like I need the money? No, for some reason, I'm being set up. Ask your auditors to verify the origin for the instructions to transfer the money into an offshore account. Also ask them to find out, if they can, when this "Swinging Dicks" account was opened. The offshore bank might not be prepared to reveal that information but I urge you to try."

"The instructions came from your account using your personal password. Explain that, unless you've given someone access to your secret and confidential details."

"At the outset you told me the auditors had not verified the authenticity of the instructions. Explain that."

The President acknowledged there was room for doubt and he'd talk to the auditors again but first he had to interview the pharmaceutical governor and the bank V.P.

Irene had been monitoring all of this and the President's latest instructions to the auditors, then the outside computer specialists arrived and set up shop in a spare office just down the corridor from her office. No introductions were made to anyone and they were the unfriendliest of people. I suppose that's the way they should be, given their job, she thought, but still…

The company auditors returned and they too kept to themselves. Irene could see from her office that no one walked between the two offices they were using. Strange that, she thought, you'd think that being on a similar mission they'd be sharing information and thoughts. Even monitoring their investigations there were no cross communications. It's almost as if there was some form of rivalry between the two firms. Maybe I could use that to further confuse what was going on she thought.

She decided to follow the route the computer specialists were taking and hacked into their website to closely follow their moves, who knows, she might learn something. They followed standard procedures then suddenly used a tricky algorithm to bring up defunct information that had traces of being used on the sites they were investigating. Very clever, she thought, very clever. That meant they were one step ahead of her and when they followed that strand it would lead right to her computer.

She smiled to herself, almost got caught out there. She was so full of her own capabilities she forgot that there was always the possibility someone else was better. That was lucky, and using some black magic with the help of the dark web, she changed her IP address. They couldn't trace her now and it taught her a valuable lesson not to be so cocky.

Then she had a thought and looked up the President's IP address. By using her original instructions to transfer the three million pounds and including his IP numbers on the dark web she was able to create that strand linking the President while still preserving the original instructions from the Treasurer pointing out him as the culprit. That's going to confuse the hell out of them.

She switched over to see how the company auditors were doing. There seemed to be general hilarity at the title the three defendants had chosen for their offshore account but despite further investigation they were no further forward. Authenticity still had to be verified. The Treasurer had already been interviewed and on the base of it, his involvement seemed inconclusive. That left the bank V.P. and the company governor still to be interviewed and either all three could be eliminated from involvement or charged with theft.

This was the report the auditors were preparing until one of their eagle-eyed team spotted the thread leading directly from the instructions to transfer the three million pounds to the offshore account. It was conclusive proof that the President was involved. Now they were puzzled. Their system did not lie, it was based on fact, however there was a slight niggle in the team leader's head, something wasn't quite right. Far be it for him to analyse any company personnel involvement, that was not his job, he now had a report to present.

He did it in such a way that he fulfilled his obligations not only to the instructions from the President but to a legal requirement to report all irregularities discovered during an official audit.

The President couldn't believe what had been put in front of him. The auditor's report, while practically duplicating the original, highlighted that until conclusive evidence could be produced from outside, formal or informal investigations, their findings still pointed to the three accused being guilty of theft on a massive scale.

In their conclusion the auditors stated that further, more detailed and precise investigations also pointed to the possible involvement of the Company President in criminal activity by being in collusion with the three defendants. They presented the link to the money transfer as proof.

To say he was poleaxed would be an understatement. He realized immediately the auditors were producing results that were incorrect. He now believed the Treasurer was innocent because he himself, was not involved in any way in the transfer of any money but now he was being accused.

He had yet to speak to the company Governor and the bank V.P. The Governor was just down the corridor so it was easy to get him to come into his office, the bank V.P. was in another building and that meeting had to be arranged for some time later. When the Governor went into the President's office, he readily admitted that he did have money problems but followed that up by pointing out that he had not used any of the £150 K that was transferred into his bank account and proclaimed his innocence of any fraud.

The President was in a quandary. It was now obvious that the allegations of theft against the three suspects was untrue but all the evidence pointed to their guilt. What on earth was he going to do if even the company auditors and the specialist auditors can't prove what is true and what isn't.

Irene had been following everything very closely and was intrigued at the attitude towards the auditor's reports.

It seemed that they had just been accepted, many questions unanswered and not even asked. She didn't see what their next step would be. Both sets of auditors had made no recommendations, stuck in their traditional black and white rolls not deviating from that traditional way of thinking. There were very few accountants and auditors who were able to break free and think for themselves. It was one thing to report a blatantly obvious illegal transfer of funds, quite another to find out why. The company auditors and the computer specialists were actually doing the company a disservice by just reporting on what they saw without delving deeper and investigating why. That was a challenge they were either not willing to, or didn't have the ability to pursue. Shame for the company, good news for Irene.

The production manager was going to have another go at using A.I. with the robots in a new manufacturing run. The President was in the control room looking at everything that was going on. The instructions had been checked and rechecked and everyone was confident the run would be trouble free and the button was pressed to start the cycle.

Irene was right on top of it and using the dark web was able to add another ingredient that would render the medicine extremely dangerous to use. She had used one of the lab technician's passwords to complete her instructions and done it about five minutes before the run was due to start. The production manager was not aware of the change because it had been slipped in using an algorithm on the dark web that made it undetectable.

Everything was running smoothly; the robots were transferring the ingredients from the storage bins according to instructions and everyone was looking quite pleased with themselves. Smiles were starting to break out then someone spoiled the atmosphere. Samples were constantly being taken for quality control and when one of the lab technicians analysed a sample his face went red and he hit the panic button. Sirens went off, lights started to flash and all the robots grounded to a halt. There was panic everywhere with the President shouting what was going on.

The production manager and lab assistants were on their computers, clicking away on their keyboards then one after the other looked at each other and shook their heads. One of them finally said,

"How in hell did that happen!" The President was shouting, "What's going on?"

When he was told, he hit the roof, he was literally raging.

"Right, he shouted, all production of everything has to cease immediately!" He turned to the production manager and said in a low threatening voice, "Find out what happened, and this time I want answers, no excuses, understand? answers!"

Irene sent anonymous messages to the world media, once again this pharmaceutical company has encountered major problems in its use of A.I. instructing robots in the manufacture of essential medicines. A near disaster was narrowly avoided by a random quality control check.

I'm winning she thought, time to up the ante. This time I'll disrupt the ordering schedule and get the inventory levels out of kilter for what was needed for the production runs. After that she thought she'd get their customers really annoyed by going into Accounts Receivable and send out demand notices for immediate payment and at the same time cancel all volume discounts previously granted by the company.

4.

GHOST GUNS

Inspector Mike O'Neil was a worried man. There had been a surge in gun crime in the past few weeks with criminals using so called "Ghost Guns ". Where the devil were they coming from? There was chatter on the streets, if you wanted a Glock 19, two thousand pounds and it was yours. Unregistered, no markings, brand new and available in a week. Place an order, cash up front and it would be delivered to your doorstep or a place of your choosing. It's almost like dealing with Amazon the Inspector thought.

The latest incident was gang related, and appeared to be a revenge shooting. The victim was having lunch at an outdoor cafe when a car pulled up and a man wearing a hoodie stepped out of the front passenger seat and walked purposely around the tables until he reached his victim. The man looked startled, shouted No! Then he was shot point blank three times. What the shooter didn't know was that two fully armed undercover police officers were having a late lunch in the cafe as it all unfolded. One of them drew his gun and yelled at the shooter to drop his weapon and put his hands in the air. The other drew his gun and raced to the front of the car that brought the shooter and shouted at the driver to turn off the engine and get out of the car. They both ignored the instructions.

The shooter turned and pointed his gun directly at the police officer who promptly pulled the trigger on his own weapon. Hit in the chest the shooter died immediately. The car driver ignored the police officer standing in front of him with a drawn pistol pointing right at him. He stupidly decided to take a chance and drove straight at him. There was no choice, he dived out of the way while letting off two shots at the driver. The car fortunately hit a lamppost and came to a halt. The driver did not survive.

It didn't take Inspector O'Neil long to arrive at the scene. It was utter chaos with police roping off sections of the street and crime scene officers recording the events as they happened. The two undercover police officers were out of sight in a police incident van giving their statements. Everything was being done to protect their identity and no pictures were allowed by the media.

The Inspector stepped into the van and shook hands with the undercover policemen. They were well experienced and one of them said, "We weren't able to apprehend them, we gave them every chance, we're just fortunate that no one else was injured. Forensics have the gun they used. It's one of those 3D printed guns. Quite remarkable the quality. It's the first one I've seen and I can't quite believe it's made out of plastic. Maybe the lab will be able to shed more light on it.

Tv crews were arriving and setting up their equipment, the whole area was being flooded by the media. The criminal's bodies were still on the street, albeit covered by tarpaulins and the scene was akin to a madhouse. The Inspector told the two undercover policemen to slip away and he would catch up with them later at the station.

For the rest of the day there was nothing else on the tv but coverage of the shooting incident. Lots of speculation about the gun used even several pictures of various 3D weapons but it was pointed out how unreliable these guns were, however it looked like someone had cracked how to make ones that were reliable and safe to use.

Like everyone else Irene was following the shooting incident on tv and couldn't help thinking about the 3D Glock 19 the lab technician James Barnes had made. I wonder she thought. The pharmaceutical company had the equipment, the expertise, and had already made one. The possibility existed that someone in the company was somehow involved in the illegal manufacture of these weapons if not James Barnes.

Now what to do. She realized the police should be informed, the information she had might be vital to their investigations but doing that would expose her and reveal her intentions. The pharmaceutical company must fall. It and their policies were responsible for her husband's death and she was determined they were not going to get away with it. She smiled to herself and thought this is the sort of dilemma that causes ulcers. Two remedies for that one, drugs, ironically drugs produced by the pharmaceutical company and two, solve the dilemma and stop worrying.

In the end she decided the way forward was a conversation with the police inspector in charge, Mike O'Neil but how to do it. She took the bull by the horns and phoned the Inspector using a disposable mobile phone. When she connected with the police station, she was told the Inspector was busy, leave a phone number and he'll get back to you. She replied, "That's going to be difficult, I have some urgent information regarding the shooting at the outdoor cafe and particularly about the 3D gun used by the assassin."

The reply was instantaneous, "Please hold the line."

In less than a minute her call was answered, "This is Inspector O'Neil I understand you have some information that might help us in our investigations into the shooting at the Cafe yesterday."

"I do, but it's going to be difficult telling you about it without revealing my identity and if that happens my cover is blown and my mission will be over."

"Are you working undercover for an agency?"

"I'm working undercover, not for an agency but for myself, on a personal matter. Quite inadvertently, I've discovered information not related to my mission but relevant to the manufacturing of 3D weapons. Problem is, the more I reveal, the more you will know and its information you need to pursue your line of inquiry and when that happens my identity will be known and I won't be able to finish what I am doing."

"We can protect you and give you a new identity"

"I appreciate that but if I accomplish my goal I shouldn't need a new identity, my real name and purpose will be revealed but not right now. Besides you might not approve of the methods I use. You can see the quandary I'm in."

"Do you think the information you have would lead to an arrest?"

"Perhaps not for this crime but an arrest for the illegal manufacture of weapons, yes absolutely."

"Okay, I have a solution. Would you trust me enough to meet up and have a talk?"

"I'm a bit hesitant at that."

"Right, tell you what, would you agree to meet one to one, a place of your choosing and a promise not to reveal any information you give me unless you approve?"

"That's asking a lot."

"I really am trustworthy you know."

"I'm thinking."

"Tell you what, it's close to lunch why don't we meet in a place of your choice, have a bite to eat and talk things over. By the way my friends call me Mikey."

He was doing his best to reassure her and it seemed to be working.

She made her decision.

"No obligations, no coercion, no commitment, my name stays with myself unless I choose otherwise. Finally, anything I reveal to you about my current investigation remains between the two of us, only the two of us. Agreed?"

"Agreed"

They had no trouble recognizing each other, apart from the descriptions they had given, they stood out as two strangers trying to link up as if they were on a blind date.

He gave a charming smile, extended his hand and said, "I'm Mikey."

She looked at him with some apprehension and replied. "I'm Irene."

She ordered a half pint of Guinness and he ordered a pint. That's a good start he thought, at least they had similar tastes.

They enjoyed a few sips in silence, getting the feel of each other then he gingerly approached the most important reason for their meeting.

"So, what do you think Irene, is there anything you'd like to talk about regarding these 3D guns or anything else for that matter, like how you found out about them. Maybe you'd like to talk about your own investigations."

"No, the reason I got in touch with you is because I inadvertently came across the blueprints in a computer system that should not be there and someone did their best to make sure they would never be discovered. I am not sure if it is an individual acting on their own, or on behalf of the company they work for."

The waiter interrupted to ask what they wanted for lunch. She chose a club sandwich so did he. Something else they have in common he thought, they like the same drink, same food, I wonder what the third thing will be.

"Can you give me any more information Irene. This sounds so promising, it's the best lead we've had so far but I can't really investigate it without more information, you do understand that, don't you?"

"Yes, I do but I'm worried that any further information I give you will lead right back to me and I would come under suspicion. That would jeopardise my investigations and my ultimate goal."

"Ok, I understand that and respect your decision. I can guess at your situation but I really need something more, something that will not implicate you in any way. If it helps, this is what I can guess at. Because you're so secretive, it's a very sensitive investigation you're on, probably personal with possible criminal implications, you don't want that interrupted or spoiled that's why you're so reluctant to tell me more but believe me, you can trust me. You probably work for the company you're investigating that's why you were able to come across this information and if they find out either that you're investigating them or divulged information to the police that puts you in a difficult situation. How am I doing so far?"

She looked at him and smiled, some of the tension in her visibly removed and said, "I guess that's why you're in the police."

They finished their lunch in silence then Irene said.

"Ok Mikey, I trust you, I work incognito at a large pharmaceutical company, which you'll find out anyway as soon as I tell you the name of the employee who made the gun using lab equipment. I'm sure you can disguise the origins of this discovery so I cannot be implicated in any way. His name is James Barnes and he is a lab technician."

Mikey looked startled.

"I know that name. I wonder if he's related to Harry Barnes. We know him as an arms merchant supplying the criminal underground but we've never been able to pin anything on him. This could be the breakthrough we've been waiting for."

He gave her the biggest smile and asked if they could meet again.

She warmed to his smile and felt she wasn't alone anymore but was still wary, he hadn't earned her full trust yet.

"Ok, I'll phone you in a week."

She smiled, shook his hand and left. He accepted she didn't give him a phone number, tell him her name or any further information. She was a very clever girl he thought, I wonder what she does. Maybe she's a private investigator. Right now, he was a very excited police Inspector as he practically raced back to his office.

Irene went back to her office with a spring in her step. She felt she now had an Ally. He had resources she did not have access to and perhaps between the two of them…

Back to reality, she had a job to do and it wasn't anything to do with working in the accounts department, she had more important things to do, this company had to fall.

She composed her letter, signed it with the President's name, headed it in bold red, FROM: ACCOUNTS RECEIVABLE

To the attention of all our customers.

It has been pointed out to me that not all of you are paying your debts within the required time frame set out in our company rules and regulations. Therefore, effective immediately, payment of your account must be made in full within one week from today.

We have also changed company policy and cancelled any existing volume discount offers effective immediately.

Signed

Thomas Jones Summerville

President.

The letter was in the system, no one questioned it, and after all it came from the president. It was mailed that day to all the company's customers. The first repercussions were instantaneous. As the letters were being mailed a copy was given to the Treasurer who read it and hit the roof. He took it in his hand and stormed into the President's office. "What on Earth were you thinking!" he shouted as he slammed the letter on his desk.

He was closely followed by the Sales Manager who also had a copy of the letter in his hand, yelling, "What in hell are you doing!"

The President read the letter and took a deep breath, "I didn't write that."

They all looked at each other. It was the Treasurer who said it first, "There's a spy in the company, a saboteur, perhaps an industrial spy. Too many things have taken place for it to be any natural event."

The Sales Manager said,

"Perhaps we've been hacked from outside, a competitor trying to give us a bad name."

The President shook his head, "There's something more going on here. This letter is just the latest attack on our company, why I don't know. Our own company auditors have examined our books extensively, in fact they've just finished and handed me their report. We've been given a clean bill of health. They can find no evidence of any hacking and they can't find anything untoward in the recent transfer of three million pounds to that offshore account, "The Swinging Dicks."

I now know the three 'Swinging Dicks' so called, was a set up, and I've had the money transferred back into the company accounts."

"I can verify that." The Treasurer said. "Thing is, the President continued, Our company auditors and the

Specialist Computer Auditors have signed off on this and found nothing wrong but I beg to differ. I feel both sets of auditors are either too lazy or too incompetent to do their job properly, especially after I gave them verbal guarantees and interrogated the three suspects."

"There is someone who has been able to create all these events without detection. This person is so good, even the auditors doubt his existence, they can't even find any trace of his interference. He is either working in the company or able to bypass all firewalls and hack into our systems. We have to find him".

The next thing Irene did was to change the ordering system for all raw materials used in the manufacture of all the company's pharmaceutical medicines. New orders were issued changing quantities and delivery dates. She used the Purchasing Department Manager's password to access the system and make the changes. They were not noticed by anyone in the department even the suppliers never questioned the changes, some quite bizarre for the ingredients involved. The changes were only noticed when the ingredients were needed to manufacture medicines and none were available in the inventory bins. Another major crisis was in the making. The President was once again raging at the incompetence of the managers involved and the lack of failsafe measures to prevent disasters like this. Deep down he knew this was another attack on the company and he resolved to find out who it was. He had to devise a trap to catch the culprit.

Irene was checking up on the lab technician James Barnes again and looking at his files using his own password. Everything looked normal until she spotted a link that shouldn't be there. He was getting careless. She followed it through the labyrinth of channels he had created to obfuscate any random or targeted search. He wasn't good enough and she was quite alarmed at what he was up to. He had downloaded an STL program from an illegal source in the U.S.A. to enable him to manufacture a 3 D printed sub machine gun. She checked the material usage for the big industrial printer and the time the machine was used for an extended period. Her hunch was right the machine was used throughout the night two nights running. My God! She thought, he made the weapon in the company lab!

She had to see Mikey. He wasn't in the office; out for the day the receptionist told her. The message she left was simple and straightforward. "Urgent I see you, same place, same time tomorrow – Irene."

When she arrived at the restaurant he was already there. He had chosen an outside table and had a pint and half a pint of Guinness sitting on the table. He must have organized it for the waiter to serve them as she arrived. He gave her a broad smile and shook her hand. She was relieved to see him and immediately felt at ease.

"Sounds like you have something important to tell me"

"You're not going to believe this."

She went on to tell him about James Barnes and the machine gun he had made in the company lab. He was incredulous and worried to say the least.

"Are you sure?"

"Positive, I can give you proof but that means revealing more of my objectives and I'm not quite ready to do that yet."

"Well from my side, I've been actively looking into the criminal empire of one Harry Barnes' cousin of the lab technician James Barnes. They are definitely in cahoots and while I can't definitely say Harry Barnes is manufacturing 3D Printed weapons, right now the latest on the streets is that you can order a Glock 19 for two thousand pounds and have it delivered in a week and if what you say is true, machine guns are next."

He'd no sooner finished talking when two black range rovers squealed to a stop at the curb drawing everyone's attention. Four men got out; evil written all over their faces. Two of them were swinging baseball bats and one was flashing a machete in the air. They headed straight for Mike O'Neil.

Mike stood up to face them and told Irene to get behind him. "Actually Mikey, I think you should get behind me."

He looked puzzled then startled when he saw the transformation taking place right in front of him. Irene's face was transformed into one of steel, her features now sharply pronounced as she turned and walked straight at the four men. She stopped in front of them and said, "Is there a problem boys?"

They were taken aback and the man not holding a weapon said, "Out of the way, this has nothing to do with you and went to push her aside, as soon as he touched her, she sprang into action. He got a swift jab to the throat followed by a sharp-edged thrust to his solar plexus. He collapsed immediately."

The second man swung his baseball bat straight at her head expecting it to connect but not expecting nothing there but thin air. Irene had somehow done a 360 degree pirouette and was now to the side of the assailant. She grabbed his arm and with one swift movement shoved it straight up and dislocated it from his shoulder and in the same movement snapped his arm breaking it at the elbow. As he doubled up in pain, she brought the edge of her hand swiftly down on the nape of his neck. He just crumpled to the floor.

The third man swung his bat wildly leaving himself wide open as the bat completing its movement went behind his back, before he could blink, he had a bloody nose, broken jaw and was lying unconscious on the ground.

Machete man was big and heavy and shouting strange incantations as he swung the machete around his head. His legs were wide apart as he was doing all this daring anyone to approach. Irene took one look, and two quick steps towards him then kicked him as hard as she could in his testicles. He went deathly white and hit the ground with a crash.

It was all over in less than two minutes. Irene said, "I hope he's already had children"

"Who the hell are you?" Irene smiled, "Another story for another time Mikey. Can you please keep me out of this, I still have a lot to do. I'm off now, be in touch."

With that she turned and walked slowly away.

The police had flooded the area and ambulances, blue lights flashing were lined up on the street. The Sergeant in charge couldn't quite believe what he was looking at. He knew the Inspector and went up to him, "Did you do all of this?"

Mike decided to keep Irene out of it as much as he could. She was a woman of mystery, that's for sure and he had to respect her request for anonymity. He would find out more about her, as it transpired, they now seemed to be working together to solve the alarming increase in "Ghost Weapons".

"I had some help. They came after me and the only case I'm really pursuing right now is Harry Barnes and his arms business. I guess he either sent them as a warning, or to take care of me permanently although if he was going to do that why not just shoot me."

The sergeant shook his head, "That wouldn't be the best idea, to shoot an Inspector in the police force. No, I reckon he sent them to teach you a lesson, instead he got taught one."

"See if you can find out who these men are and if you can trace them back to Harry Barnes. I'm going to the office now. For the media, the statement is, the criminal underworld attempted to injure a police officer in his line of duty and investigations are ongoing."

When he got to the office a package had been delivered for his attention. It was from Irene with a copy of the blueprint for the machine gun and proof of its manufacture at the pharmaceutical company's lab. The note simply said, I was going to give you this earlier but things got out of hand pretty quickly. I'll be in touch… it was signed. Irene.

Mike was in his Superintendent's office giving him an update of his investigations into Harry Barnes. He told him he had an informer who was helping him out and she was already heavily involved in her own investigations and luckily her case and his were linked so she was able to give him information he did not have. The only stipulation was that she was only to be known to me and not revealed to anyone else.

Do you trust her Mike? "With my life"

"I hear rumours that a woman was involved in that fracas at the restaurant today. Is that her?"

"Yes, it is, and if it hadn't been for her, I might have been in real trouble."

"Ok Mike sounds like you've got everything under control. Remember if I can be of any help, I'm only a phone call away."

"Thank you, I'll keep you informed."

He gathered his team together, "Right people, do we have the names of the four idiots who attacked me and can we link them to Harry Barnes, if we don't have that information yet, concentrate on getting it. We also have the two range rovers they used, find out what you can about them."

Mike did not believe in formalities and everyone was on a first name basis. One of the team said, "Mike, we understand there was a girl involved in the fight at the restaurant can you tell us anything about that?"

"Yes, she is an informant and doesn't want to be named because she is working on another investigation and is deep undercover. I have given her assurances that nothing will be revealed about her or what her work is. I am the only person who knows anything about her, okay?"

"Okay, understood, but is it true she's the one who took care of the four criminals?"

"Much as I'd like to take the credit, yes it's true and to be honest, if she hadn't been there, the confrontation might have ended quite differently."

"So, is she some kind of Lara Croft?"

That brought a few laughs, "Wouldn't that be nice. We keep all of this to ourselves and don't talk it up if someone mentions it. She wants to remain low key and basically undercover. Is that ok with everyone?"

There was a chorus of "understood."

"Right then, let's see if we can crack this one."

It was a week after the incident and they finally had a result. One of Mike's assailants was now identified as working for Harry Barnes. He was the one with no weapons and appeared to be in charge. The two bat swingers and machete man couldn't be traced and appeared to be street fodder picked up for a one-off job. They were all in hospital, some worse off than others. Mike decided to visit the leader who was called Diddly Jones.

He wasn't the arrogant, swaggering gangster anymore. He was propped up in his bed with a drip coming out of his arm and hooked up to a machine that continuously beeped and flashed red signals.

"We'll Diddly, didn't turn out the way you expected did it."

It was a rhetorical question and he just stared at Mike and said in a rasping voice, "Your time is coming and sooner than you think."

"Are you threatening a police officer?"

Mike looked carefully around, couldn't see any nurses and covered Diddly's mouth with his left hand and with the fingers of his right slowly pressed them into his solar plexus where Irene had hit him. Diddly writhed and groaned while kicking his feet around. Mike pulled his hand away and said, "What a coward, you need three armed men to back you up, not brave enough to do it yourself are you. Threaten me will you…keep this in your tiny little mind… your cards are marked and you don't have much time left at all and that's not a promise, it's fact. Now tell me, did your boss order the attack on me?"

Diddly said nothing and Mike left the room.

Back at the office, one of his men had taken the initiative and ordered a Glock 19 on the street and was told to have his two thousand pounds ready in a fortnight. He questioned the length of time and was told they were busy with a lot of orders. The policeman hadn't disguised himself, just changed into work clothes and approached someone they were pretty sure was involved. They were so greedy, no questions were asked, they had no vetting process they just accepted the order. The officer said, "Frankly Mike, I didn't really expect anything to come out of it that's why I never ran it past you first, I hope you don't mind."

"No problem, John, this could be a breakthrough for us, good work. We'll have to be very careful how we handle this."

"Ok, different angle now, were going to put surveillance on Harry Barnes's house. It's at the edge of town, a large property with a lot of land and he's recently had a large shed built on it with a high voltage phase 3 line going in. I'm betting that shed is where he is making these guns. I want a list of all vehicles going in and out of that house. Is anyone here licensed to operate a drone?"

One detective put up her hand, "I am."

Everyone turned to look at her somewhat surprised. Liz Smith was a popular member of the team and she was someone who kept her own counsel. No one knew much about her and she liked to keep it that way. She looked about her and made a decision.

"This just might come out now that I've declared myself. I've been a detective for just over three years now and really enjoy the work. I like to think I'm good at it and the camaraderie in this team makes me feel right at home."

"Here goes, in a previous life I used to be a pilot in the R.A.F. I've flown all types of planes, seems I have a natural ability and I also flew drones on missions I'm not allowed to talk about. I know you now have a thousand questions but I have a simple request. Like yourselves I've signed the Official Secrets Act so I'm not allowed to talk about my life before I joined the police force. Can we please respect that and keep it to yourselves. Everyone looked around, finally someone said, "Well you kept that pretty quiet, no reason why it shouldn't remain that way although I must say you are a bit of a dark horse, have you got any other surprises for us?"

"No, that's it and thank you all, this means a lot to me."

Mike said, "Thanks for sharing that, Liz. Before we go on, does anyone else want to enlighten us with secrets from their past?"

Silence for a while then someone piped up, "I used to be a drummer in a boy band, we were so bad it folded after two concerts." Someone shouted,

"What was its name? I just might have heard of it."

"We called ourselves, 'The Golden Pelicans' we were dressed all in gold with Pelican hats."

There was instant laughter.

"Thanks for sharing that Frank" said Mike with a smile on his face, how old were you?

"A pubescent sixteen."

More laughter then Mike took control again.

"Liz, the police force has several drones they use I want you to choose the one you want. If nothing is suitable let me know. I want a view where the drone will not be noticed and if need be, the ability to follow vehicles or people. Something that will give us a sharp picture."

"Right Mike, I know just the drone for the job, I'll see what they have and get back to you."

"Okay, we have to set up a surveillance on Harry Barnes not just his house. I want to know where he is at any given time. Does anyone have any idea where he is right now?"

"I take it from the deafening silence that's a no. So, let's get moving and find out."

Irene had gone back to the office at the pharmaceutical company intent on checking further into Harry' Barnes's cousin James and what was going on in the experimental lab. She hacked into the lab account using the production manager's password. Management had introduced new anti-virus software and a more sophisticated firewall that must have been set up by the computer specialists. It was a bit more complicated to get around but not impossible. James Barnes had also made it a bit more difficult to get into any of the lab accounts but she was also able to work her way through the myriad of obstacles he had engineered to keep the information secret.

The more she looked at what was in the archives the faster her heart began to beat. My God, Mikey has to know about this. She started printing blueprints for sub machine guns but didn't want to stay on line too long in case she was discovered. She carefully logged out and was sure she had covered her footsteps.

The operator said that Inspector O'Neill was out of the office, leave a message and he would get back to you. It was then that Irene realized she had to change her way of thinking. She had to be able to contact him at any time. Perhaps it was time to reveal who she really was and what she was doing. She left a message for him to call her a.s.a.p. And left her burner phone number.

She did some more research and found that the blueprints were for an FGC9 sub machine gun which apparently was the most capable 3-D printed firearm currently designed. It also circumvents European firearm regulations by avoiding the use of regulated component parts. The gun is 80% plastic and the barrel, spring and other metal parts are generally available to legally buy in most hardware shops. If Harry Barnes has the facilities and the equipment, coupled with the expertise of his cousin James he could very well be mass manufacturing these guns. She had to see Mikey. The previous blueprint she had given him was for a completely different machine gun.

The drone that Liz had in mind wasn't used by the police force but was ideal for the surveillance Mike had in mind. She explained to him that military use drones had higher specs than those used by civilians and she still had contacts in the air force. The possibility existed that with her record and background they could borrow one until the operation was over.

"Great Liz, you get me the name to contact for permission and I'll get the Superintendent to put in a request."

It didn't take long, apparently Liz was highly thought of, had a string of medals and commendations and the military said the police could borrow the drone she wanted for as long as was needed. Liz would be stationed at the nearest military air field and fly the drone from there. She would be in constant radio contact with Mike. The next few days were spent setting up systems, testing the drone and its suitability with a few test runs. The military recognized the need to put a halt to the manufacture of these so called "Ghost guns" and were fully behind Mike and the police in putting an end to it before it fully got into production.

The team was quite excited that one of their members was the pilot flying the drone and knew exactly what was needed and could therefore practically work independently. Trial runs were over and they were fully operational. What Liz never told Mike was that this drone had the capability to not only fly at night but still produce almost crystal-clear images. There were certain military secrets best left that way. This ability gave them unequalled advantages and Liz decided to keep that to herself unless there was a situation that she absolutely had to reveal all.

Mike got the message from Irene and was concerned at her sense of urgency. He phoned right away and arranged to meet at a local pub. He could go right away but she had to wait until lunch before she could leave the office. She'd been worried about how much she should tell him about her own situation and in the end decided as little as possible – just enough to satisfy him.

It was lunchtime and it was busy but he had been able to get a table for them. He got there first and could see how anxious she was as soon as she arrived. She was clutching a large brown envelope tightly to her chest and he knew it must be important. They shook hands and he nodded at a waiter to order some drinks and lunch.

"Now, you look rather stressed-out Irene, what's been happening?"

"I had to see you right away, I checked into what our friend James Barnes has been up to. He's put extra controls on his files to prevent infiltration but I was able to bypass them and print out his latest blueprints. I made copies for you. These are plans for sub machine guns that can be manufactured from 3D printers. They are different machine guns from the blueprints I gave you earlier. He's either trying them all out to decide which is the best or going all out to make them and give the criminal underworld a choice of weapon."

"Irene, I can't believe what you've done, this is incredible thank you so much. I'll get our boys checking out these blueprints right away. It actually ties in with what we are doing. Harry Barnes has just built a large shed in his garden, capable of manufacturing hand guns and machine guns. We believe that's exactly what he is doing and we have now got his house under surveillance 24 hours a day."

They didn't talk much during lunch. Mike was hoping Irene would open up some more about herself but she wasn't forthcoming so he decided to broach the subject before she had to return to her office.

"You know Irene, I'd love to know more about you but I understand your reticence at revealing too much as you are working deep undercover but here's a situation where you wanted to get in touch immediately but weren't able to. We got there in the end but I would feel more comfortable if we had instant communication between us, what do you say?"

"I'm starting to feel the same Mikey and I still don't want to tell you everything, not yet anyway, I'm sure you won't agree with my methods. I'm not worried about that, just what it will reveal before I'm finished. Rest assured I will tell you everything, you just have to be patient. One request and it involves a solemn promise. Anything I tell you must remain just between the two of us, only the two of us. Can you give me that assurance?"

Without hesitation Mikey immediately put out his hand, looked Irene directly in her eyes and said, "Of course I can, rest assured."

They shook hands and smiled at each other. What they weren't aware of was that four members of his team were also having lunch in the same pub and saw everything that went on. They didn't hear what was said but they all agreed this was the mysterious "Lara Croft". Question now was whether they should let themselves be known or not. A quick discussion and they all agreed that if the boss had already decided not to tell the team anything about the mysterious woman, it was for a reason, and they quietly slipped out of the pub.

"Right, said Irene, some basic information. I use a burner phone because I don't want my real identity known and I'll continue with that number until I find it necessary to get a new phone at which time, I will tell you. I also need a phone number that I can contact you twenty-four seven. I work in the accounts department of the pharmaceutical company I'm investigating. Of course, they are not aware of who I am and what I'm doing. I'm not working for anyone."

This is my own investigation and it is personal, very personal so I have to be very careful I am not discovered. I have made preparations for an instant exit if needed. I am a Forensic accountant and an Insolvency Expert. I have particular skills in computer technology and can manipulate my way through the "Dark Web" I also have a black belt, 5th Dan in Karate and I have several classes I teach. No one knows of that particular skill and one day I will tell you all about it.

It was just by chance I discovered what James Barnes was up to and with these latest blueprints I checked inventory levels and he ordered a lot of particularly hard plastic for use in a 3D Printer. He's used the lot and checking his work schedule he has practically worked through the night two nights running. That plastic is not used for anything else. Like all companies they are getting used to manufacturing their own spare parts and I'm sure that he used the plastic to make at least two of the latest type of sub machine guns. He's a senior member of staff, practically runs the lab and is in charge of the experimental lab that uses A.I. As an aside, I've been able to screw up two of his applications to use A.I. in a manufacturing run for different medicines.

The company was not too happy about that, no one claimed responsibility and they brought in a team of computer specialists to find out what went wrong. I put the blame on the Production Manager and he's still denying it.

There's lots of things I can do to mess them up but the big one has yet to come. Right now, I'm trying to discover if any of the management team is involved in any way with these "Ghost Guns".

That's all for now Mikey, send me your phone number, I'd better get back before I'm missed and they start asking questions.

He was gob smacked. Couldn't quite believe how this person had just appeared out of nowhere at a crucial point in his investigation into Harry Barnes. She had a social conscience and was providing so much information and most important of all, as far as he was concerned, she had saved his skin in that confrontation at the outdoor cafe. He couldn't share the information she'd just told him; he'd given a solemn promise. Irene whatever her name, was a mystery woman, in the words of his team, a modern-day Lara Croft. She was now crucial to his investigations.

His mobile phone started making alarm bell signals increasing in crescendo with each ring. He frowned and left the pub that meant there was an emergency. Outside, he called the office and was told that the drone operator urgently wanted to talk to him. Breathless when he reached the office, he looked at the live pictures being relayed by the drone and spoke at the console which was live for two-way conversations.

"Yes Liz, it's Mike, what's happening?"

"You see the two vans in the picture, they left Harry Barnes's house at great speed one after the other. They are travelling in tandem and from their route I can project that they are heading for Manchester. I think that it would be a fair assumption that they have a cargo of recently manufactured "Ghost Guns" and they should be intercepted either immediately or wait till they reach their destination and arrest the recipients as well. If you decide on the latter, I have no problem following them, I'm flying at twenty thousand feet so there is no way they can tell they are being followed from the air."

My problem is air traffic over Manchester and once they are in the city there are many ways, they can escape observation. If you ask my opinion, I'd intercept sooner rather than later. Big decision now Mike, we've got time to organize an ambush, I can scout ahead and pick a spot. Here's an interesting thought, if I had a couple of rockets attached there would be no question of who would be worse off. Maybe it's something we should discuss. In my experience the future is variable and it is better to be prepared for all eventualities. Mind you to go armed would probably mean getting the M.O.D. Involved and while you could present a legitimate case it would probably be an uphill battle to get it approved. However, given the seriousness of 3D printed weapons, which is on the verge of becoming an epidemic just look at the problems the police have in the States and in my opinion, they stupidly legitimized the manufacture of these weapons so you could say they are the author of their own misfortunes. We really have to clamp down on that ever happening in the U.K. and here endeth my lesson for the day."

"Interesting Liz, we'll have to get together and talk about this some more. Right now, I agree with you we have to intercept these vans without too much delay. You scout around and see the best spot for an ambush and I'll organize the reception committee. The vans are close enough that our team can probably get involved although it would probably be prudent to get 'Armed Response' as well. I'll stay on an open line, get back to me when you work something out."

This was something new for the detectives and those who were in the office followed everything as Mike and Liz talked their way through the developments as they unfolded. There was now a general buzz of excitement running through the team as they had never been involved in something like this before and to think it was one of their team who was flying the drone. Mike said, "Come on folks let's hit the road."

As they left the office one of them shouted, "Go Liz!" That was followed by a chorus of cheers.

Mike kept his Superintendent informed and that one of his team was a pilot and flying the drone. He was staggered to say the least and decided it best to let the Chief Constable know what was happening because it wasn't the normal type of operation they set up and if it was successful, they would put a stop to the mass production of a dangerous new type of weapon.

Mike and his team were in two cars speeding up the motorway on the way to a rendezvous with an armed response team. Liz had identified a section of highway going through a National Park that seemed ideal for an intervention. Time was still on their side and they should be able to get set up before the two vans reached them.

Liz came through the communication system they had hastily set up.

"The two vans have pulled into a lay-by. Four men are out, two from each van looks like a pit stop." She laughed, if they only knew the definition this drone's camera was capable of...

The trap was set and as the two vans approached one of Mike's vehicles pulled out from behind a hedge and blocked the road. As the vans stopped Mike's other vehicle pulled out and blocked any reversal. The armed response unit then came out of the foliage and surrounded both vans. Guns drawn, they shouted at the occupants to get out of their vehicles with their hands in the air. Startled, they did as they were told. A quick personal search uncovered three Glock-19 hand guns. They were the real McCoy, no plastic involved here.

Hands behind their backs they were handcuffed and cautioned. They were professional criminals, to a man, when questioned the reply was the same.

"No comment."

Mike and his team opened the van doors and found both vehicles full of wooden crates. They looked at each other and Mike said, "Moment of truth."

They took the first box out, laid it on the ground and prized open the lid. There, laid side by side were four sub machine guns all made out of plastic and that was just the first layer. There were three layers, a total of twelve guns per box. There were six boxes in each van, a grand total of 144 sub machine guns.

The armed response leader shook his head, couldn't believe it, neither could Mike and his team. This was a major find and they just prevented the criminal underworld from being armed with the most dangerous of all weapons.

The four men were formally arrested and charged with possession of banned weapons. They were taken away by the police to a station not used for the ordinary criminal and were about to receive the attention of some very unpleasant people. Mike arranged for another team of armed police officers to take possession of the vans and their contents and have them properly tested and examined.

The next thing Mike did was contact Liz. The line was still open, "We did it Liz, or maybe I should say you did it. The two vans had 144 sub machine guns, all made with plastic. We are heading back to the office just now to check in and give a brief report. Then we are going to the pub to celebrate and I want you there. We have a few hours can you make it?"

"Yes, Mike I'll be there."

"One other thing, don't return the drone yet we haven't finished with Harry Barnes."

When they reached the office Mike sent a short message to Irene, "Get in touch - good news."

His phone rang before he could get up from his desk, "What's up?"

Irene's voice was quiet almost a whisper, "I'm still in the office, people around but I thought it might be important."

"It is, we just intercepted two vans leaving Harry's place, on the way to Manchester, they had 144 sub machine guns, thought you would like to know as you had a major part in this breakthrough. The team is heading to the pub to celebrate, any chance you could join us? Before you say no keep in mind no one knows who you are or what you do. You are probably the most important member of this team and I think you should meet everyone without letting them know who you are. We could make up a story, say you are liaison from head office coordinating all information for management. What do you say, I think it's important, you've been under a lot of stress, you need to relax and here's the ideal opportunity… want to think about it and call me back? You need the break, call me."

Mike went into the Superintendent's office where he was met with a big smile and a warm handshake, "Well done Mike, you've pulled together a great team. I told the Chief Constable what you've done and he's on his way here right now to congratulate everyone. This is a major breakthrough do you know who's making them?"

"I do and that is the next operation. There is more to come but I don't want to reveal too much until we get all the dots in place, if it all comes together, you're going to get the surprise of your life and that's all I can say right now."

They were interrupted by wild cheering; Liz had just arrived. The Superintendent looked quizzically at Mike; eyebrows raised.

"That's Liz our drone pilot and a detective in our team. If you'll excuse me, in fact come out and meet her and the rest of the team."

Introductions were made and there was such a feeling of camaraderie, everyone talking at once then the door opened and the Chief Constable walked in. There was immediate silence to which he said, don't stop just because I arrived. I came here to congratulate everyone, what a result! We haven't had success like this for a long time. He went on to have a brief chat with each and every one of them and assured Liz her little secret would stay that way. A special talk was reserved for Mike who simply said we are a team and work well together.

The Chief Constable said, "I presume you will all be going out for a drink to celebrate?"

"As soon as you leave."

"Enjoy yourselves, you deserve it and as a thank you for such hard work and a brilliant result, all drinks are on the department."

Mike smiled, shook hands and went out to have a talk with everyone and let them know the Chief Constable was paying. Another cheer rang out. Then his phone rang. It was Irene, she had decided to join everyone but was worried about her cover story. Mike told her to say she was the liaison officer at head office and she was a civilian. She was just putting everything together for a report about the whole operation and to stick close to him. He told her it was the last pub they had met for a drink. He would stick close to the door and wait for her. Last thing, don't worry we're a friendly bunch. By the way the Chief Constable just left and he's footing the bill. See you shortly.

The pub had never been so busy, when word spread that the Chief was paying it was all hands to the deck so to speak. Mike was finding it difficult to exclude people not on his team from having a free drink because they were friends and relied on each other at different times. In the end he said, "What the hell" and it was an open bar.

Irene slipped in and looked around the room at the same time as Mike was scanning everyone hanging around the door. Their eyes made contact at the same time and both broke into wide smiles. Mike walked up to her and guided her to his immediate team. "Glad you came, now just relax and enjoy yourself. Is it a Guinness or something else?"

"A Guinness would be fine thank you."

There were six of his team including Liz and he introduced Irene as the liaison officer from Head Office who was here to write a report on the operation just completed. Irene took the initiative and said it must be very rewarding to put the work in and get the best possible results at the end of the day. I know you will all be writing up your own reports and I look forward to reading them. Just now it's idle chit chat and reliving the experience. It's great to get together and rehash what just happened.

Mike appeared with Irene's drink and they started talking about the clarity of the pictures beamed down from the drone. Liz started fidgeting and not volunteering any information at which point Mike interjected and explained to Irene, this is confidential and within the team we have given our word not to discuss it with anyone. Liz as well as being a detective on our team, in a previous life was a pilot in the R.A.F. and she was our pilot operating the drone. There, that should get any awkwardness out of the way.

Irene picked up right away and said of course I understand and rest assured my mouth is shut and any reference I make about the drone will simply be that a drone was used to get as much information as possible. Everyone visibly relaxed and the conversation became less stilted. A few drinks later there was more laughter, more familiarity, more questions.

Two of the detectives were looking closely at Irene and whispering to each other, one said, "I'd swear that Irene is 'Lara Croft', the woman Mike was having a drink with right here the other day."

"She might well be, but we are saying nothing, absolutely nothing. If Mike wanted us to know he'd tell us. He has his reasons and we should respect that. Besides I like my job and I like working for Mike and I am doing nothing to jeopardize that and neither are you. Understood!"

Irene was getting to know Liz and finding out about life as a pilot. She found it absolutely fascinating the different uses a plane had and the adaptations that were made to enable them to perform a specific function. Liz had spent several months as a bush pilot in Canada flying the De Havilland Beaver, designed and built to use skis, floats and wheels and the Cessna 180 that had a speed of 150 mph. Both planes were made to give access to the communities in the vast northern areas where no roads existed but there were many communities scattered all over the country. There were hundreds of lakes and with floats you could land where needed and in the winter with skis and so much snow you could land anywhere. She had some great stories and they said they would get together and talk about them over a drink or two once things had quietened down at work.

Irene knew she had a few hurdles to jump over before she was able to relax enough to socialize again. She still had a lot of unfinished business at the pharmaceutical company.

Celebrations were winding down and people were starting to leave and head home. Irene and Mike were standing together as the team left shouting,

"Thanks Boss" Mike shouted back, "See you tomorrow, probably a little later than normal, just don't push it" and he smiled. Everyone got it and gave a wave as they left, some a little worse than others.

Irene looked at Mike.

"I can see you're a good boss and that's why you've got the team you have. It also looks like, inadvertently, I have become a member as well."

She smiled at him and said, "I had a good time, thanks for insisting I come along. I'd better get moving as well. "Will you be alright or will I get a taxi for you?"

"Thanks, but I'll be okay."

She gave him a smile and a light hug and said I'll be in touch.

James Barnes was a worried man. His cousin had phoned him to tell him about the police interception and the loss of all the machine guns he had just manufactured. Harry was furious, figured there was a spy or an informant in his organization. He had taken every precaution and couldn't understand how the police knew, first of all, about the machine guns and secondly how they were able to know their location when they sprang their trap.

At the present time no one had approached his house, it didn't seem to be under surveillance, he had installed CCTV equipment and he had an operator monitoring all the screens around the clock. There had been no movement, no intruders so a real mystery, an expensive mystery. He was starting to think a rival gang had infiltrated his operation.

James had told Harry to cool it for a while as they tried to figure it out but he was the impetuous type and wanted to continue with production now that he had the manufacturing line working smoothly. He wouldn't be told and James could see trouble on the horizon.

Back in his lab he reviewed everything that had happened since he first made the Glock.

He was positive he had covered his tracks. Harry had done all the right things but still the police had found out about the guns and were able to intercept the shipment. There has to be something else he was missing. There had been quite a few problems as of late in the company, production problems, getting A.I. to work with the robots, the V.P. being fired for taking backhanders, two security guards being beaten up, supposed embezzlement of 3 million pounds, Interpol being called in, a special audit being made and a specialist computer company called in.

There was definitely something going on. It was almost as if the company was being targeted, too many things were happening and now Harry's shipment had been intercepted. Perhaps they were being hacked but surely the auditors or the computer specialists would have discovered that. The only other possibility was that someone already working for the company was doing the damage but if it was the same person how did he cotton on to Harry and get his shipment intercepted. He was going to have to do a lot of thinking and be ultra careful.

5.

INSHALLAH

Irene was deep in thought. Her primary objective was to punish those responsible for bringing about her husband's death and ultimately destroying the pharmaceutical company. However, she had been waylaid by the discovery of James Barnes and his secretive and illegal gun making. Mikey seemed to have that under control so she decided to concentrate on her original objective.

Something she had never thought about before was the shareholders. Who actually owned the company so she hacked her way into the Balance Sheet and discovered it was a private limited company primarily owned by three shareholders the largest called Inshallah. That got her interest right away. She understood it was an Arabic word in the Muslim faith that basically meant, If God Wills it. Don't tell me the company is owned and controlled by Arabs she thought. That opens up all kinds of possibilities. It could quite easily be legitimate but why choose a word in the Muslim faith for ownership of a company, why not something innocuous that would not bring attention to it. The name had all kinds of connotations.

She investigated deeper into "Inshallah" and the sole owner was a Sheikh Faisal from Saudi Arabia. The forensic accountant in her would not let it rest there, going deeper she discovered that he was a distant cousin of Osama Bin Laden and a member of Al-Qaeda. My God, she thought, can it get any worse. She kept going and yes, it did get worse. Pharmaceutical companies created a lot of wealth and in the last year issued the shareholders with a massive bonus. The "Inshallah" share was 100 million pounds. An amount she could hardly believe and this was on top of his share of profits. She kept going. The money was transferred to an account in Venezuela. She could only guess that with his background in Al-Qaeda, the deep political and financial crisis the country was in, his money was going towards starting a revolution. The rewards were great, Venezuela possessed the world's largest crude oil reserve and if he could be successful in staging a coup, he and presumably his cohorts would have access to untold wealth.

She sat back for a minute. *Am I right in my thinking?* Thought it through again and reached the same conclusion. What have I stumbled into she thought. To seek revenge for the death of her husband she got a job in the pharmaceutical company he worked in, found corruption, illegal manufacturing of so called "Ghost

Weapons" and now a connection to a possible government overthrow. With one dubious owner, was the company even legal. She decided to investigate the other two shareholders. Once she had those answers, she had to run it all past Inspector Mike O'Neill.

It didn't take her long to get answers for the other two shareholders. They were all related, one was a brother, the other a cousin. They all had the same background and their bonuses while considerably lower all went to the same bank account in Venezuela. It made her think more about the President and the role he had to play, apart from running the company. Time for an in-depth investigation into Mr. Thomas Jones Summerville.

He was born in Liverpool and grew up the hard way, got involved in gangs, was arrested twice but never charged. He had brains however and that lead him to University in Durham where he graduated with an MBA degree. From there he was enticed to work in Saudi Arabia. He worked there for ten years where he studied languages part time and is fluent in Arabic. That was the connection. He must have met Sheikh Faisal there, a distant cousin of Osama bin laden. The Bin Laden family fortune is in the billions.

Irene was starting to think that what she was uncovering was pretty far-fetched but the facts were there. On looking into Osama bin Laden, she found that he had left 29 million dollars in his will to be used for jihad. So, it appeared to be in the family psyche.

She went over it again. The pharmaceutical company was owned by three shareholders, all related and all in the Bin Laden family, one of the richest families in Saudi Arabia worth billions. Thomas Jones Summerville met the Bin Ladens when he worked in Saudi and it surely was no coincidence that he was now the President of the company that was started shortly after he returned to the U.K. They apparently had affiliated pharmaceuticals in other countries. Her mind was starting to run overtime, if all these pharmaceutical companies were owned by members of the Bin Laden family and company bonuses were sent to an account in Venezuela, perhaps the same account that Sheikh Faisal had sent his bonus to. That money could not be traced to the Bin Ladens it was very clever how they had done it. If she was right the money in that account was building up to start a revolution in Venezuela and Osama's final wish could be on the horizon.

Time to become more proactive. She was going to see if she could force the President into doing something really stupid and at the same time verify if she was barking up the wrong tree with her conspiracy theory.

She started by creating an account on the Web calling it "Retribution" and gave its home address as, The Blue Skies up above. All of this was done on the dark web and with her I.T. skills was able to make sure nothing could be traced back to her. Next, she sent Mr. Thomas Jones Summerville a message from the "Retribution" account – Your past is about to catch up with you. Think of all the evil things you have done in your life then know that the result of your most heinous crime is about to visit you. Signed: Nemesis, she sent copies to the Treasurer, Sales Manager, I.T. Manager and Sheikh Faisal.

Then she sent a message to Sheikh Faisal: I know what you are up to, you would be wise to look over your shoulder. Signed: Nemesis.

She sent copies to the President Mr Thomas Jones Summerville, the Treasurer, Sales Manager and the I.T. Manager.

Irene checked into the Lab Account to see if any unusual activity had been going on and any purchase of high strength plastic that could be used in the manufacture of "Ghost Weapons". Everything seemed to be normal and the production manager had introduced controls to constantly monitor stock levels. They were about to do another trial run using AI with the robots. She wanted to create as many diversions as possible so the company would experience attacks on different fronts.

On another level, she sent James Barnes a message from the "Retribution Account" it simply said: I know what you did. Signed: Nemesis and sent a copy to the President.

She didn't want everything to drag on and now knew enough about the company, the venture into "Ghost Guns" and the possible attack on the Venezuelan Government to move everything up a notch. All she had to do was sit tight and be ready to make a hasty exit if it all "Went to shit".

Mike had authorized Liz to keep up surveillance on Harry Barnes for another week. His judgment was rewarded well before the week was up. Liz noticed increased activity at the newly built barn. Trucks were arriving and crates of material were being unloaded and taken indoors. She was still cruising at 20 thousand feet and recording what was happening with the drone's cameras.

There was a flurry of activity and Harry Barnes came out of the shed holding on to what looked like a sub machine gun. A group of his men gathered around and he appeared to be showing it off and passing it around. He had apparently sound proofed his shed and all testing and target practice was done indoors. Why he chose to bring it outside was a mystery to Liz and she was able to use the advanced camera technology to take close up pictures of the weapon so that it could be properly identified. She then put in an urgent call to Mike. It was answered almost immediately.

"What's happening Liz?"

"Mike look at the monitor, Harry Barnes is outside showing off what appears to be a new machine gun.

Hopefully someone will be able to identify it. Why he's doing that I have no idea, maybe he's just plain stupid."

"I'd agree with you there Liz. I'll get these pictures to the right people. Well done."

"Do you want me to continue surveillance?"

"Definitely, you've been fantastic so far. We'll catch up soon."

Mike took the pictures into the Superintendent's office, "Looks like we might have another problem with our friend Harry Barnes only this time we have the proof. Liz has been able to get pictures of him outside his shed showing off a machine gun to his gang. I've forwarded pictures to forensics to see if they can identify the weapon. It's one of the so called "Ghost Guns" made out of plastic using a computer printout on a 3D Printer."

"My God, how the world has changed, some of this stuff nowadays is pure science fiction, guns made out of plastic, where will it end. Well done, Mike, looks like we're finally going to be able to put Mr. Harry Barnes away for a long time."

Mike then sent a message to Irene bringing her up to date and asking if she knew if the cousin James had any involvement in this latest activity.

Irene replied almost immediately. "I've just finished monitoring his accounts and looks like he is lying low, probably trying to distance himself from his cousin after you seized all those weapons. There is however something that could be of major importance I have to talk to you about. I've been holding off until certain events I've put in place show some results and I'm expecting that to happen any time. When it does, I'll get in touch."

"You have me intrigued, can't wait to hear from you, Mikey."

It was starting to kick off. The President had hastily called a meeting. The entire cabal was present including, the Treasurer, the Sales Manager, the I.T. Manager and the Lab Technician James Barnes. James had no idea why he was called to a senior management meeting. He also had no idea the others had received messages from someone calling themselves "Nemesis" or the contents of those messages. He was more concerned about the one he had received. It could only refer to the guns he had made in the lab although how "Nemesis", whoever that was, had found out about his secret was a mystery to him. Because - copy to President- was marked on his message he presumed that was why he was invited to the meeting, to explain himself, but if he told the truth, trying not to implicate his cousin he was sure he would go straight to jail. He was in a quandary not knowing how to respond.

The President didn't look his normal self, more like a deeply worried man with the weight of the world on his shoulders. The rest of the management team looked like it was their last supper. They had just sat down when the

President's secretary rushed in to which he rather crossly said,

"I told you no interruptions!"

"It's Sheikh Faisal – he's pretty upset".

"Thomas Jones Summerville groaned, shook his head and said, "I'll take it in my office."

Then told everyone to stay put, he was sure it was about the messages they had all received.

"So, what the hell is going on over there? Who is Nemesis? What does he know and how did he find out?"

Sheikh Faisal had fallen for Irene's message.

"This has come out of the blue. I have no idea who this "Nemesis" is or what he knows. I'll get extra I.T. people in to trace the origin of these messages."

"Everything we have done is legal even the shareholder's choice of transferring their bonus to wherever we want."

"Yes, that's true but if Nemesis knows the shareholder's bonus is transferred to Venezuela there might be questions why."

"Quite simply, I have other business interests there."

"What you have to remember is that if "Nemesis" has been able to get this far, he has more and is holding back to see your reaction. What he wants I do not know but we are about to have a special meeting to try and work it out. Don't be surprised if you hear more from the person calling himself "Nemesis" and don't forget that the word stands for retribution for evil deeds. You have to ask yourself if you fit in that category. Have you done something to cause this person to rise against you. Only you have the answer to that. I have the feeling this is just the beginning. I have to get to this meeting, keep in touch. Ma'a salama."

What Mr. Thomas Jones Summerville should also be asking is what he and the pharmaceutical company have done to raise the spectre of an avenging "Nemesis".

They held up the meeting until the President returned. Until then, they talked amongst themselves. The management team asked the lab technician what he was doing there as he was the odd man out. James Barnes gritted his teeth and told them he had no idea; he had just been invited by the President.

Thomas Jones Summerville took his place at the table, looked around and said, "This company is in serious trouble. We have someone called 'Nemesis' sending messages full of innuendo and we have problems within the company for example disruptions in manufacturing, Interpol investigating us, having to order two special audits. It seems the list is growing daily. The only conclusion I can reach is that someone is trying to destroy this company. We have to find who and why this is happening. For those of you who don't know, there are three people who set this company up and own it outright. The largest shareholder is Sheikh Faisal and he is based in Saudi Arabia. That was him on the phone just now, not a happy man, he has just been threatened by Nemesis as well. It would appear past indiscretions are being put into play and I want your thoughts on it.

Let's start with you James. I received a copy of the message Nemesis sent you - I know what you did – what is that all about?"

James had thought this through, for sure he would go to jail if it ever came out what he had done so he had nothing to lose by denying anything untoward had happened in his past. They would have to prove it and he was confident enough in his own abilities that it would not be discovered. The one niggle was that someone knew something.

"I have no idea. I've searched my memory and can only come up with the thought that he is grasping at straws trying to unnerve us, throw anything at us to make us start doubting ourselves and make us question each other and create dissent within the company."

"But why would he choose you a lab technician. You do your work in the lab and have nothing to do with running the company why would Nemesis target you? Any thoughts anyone? Everyone here has been targeted so what is the common denominator?"

He had to stop it there because his secretary had once again interrupted the meeting,

"It's Sheikh Faisal again, said he is on the way here and you had better have some answers ready for him."

"Great, that's all we need. Right, everyone get your thinking caps on, from memory this guy can be a nasty bit of work. In retrospect maybe this "Nemesis" has been able to get something on him. If anyone comes up with anything come and see me right away."

What the President didn't tell anyone was that while he worked in Saudi Arabia, he came under the influence of Sheikh Faisal and was promised millions, deposited in a Saudi bank account that only he would know about if he set up and operated a pharmaceutical company. What Thomas Jones Summerville didn't know was the Sheikh's ulterior motive. Irene had worked that out and unsure of herself had set a trap that had now been sprung.

Irene had been monitoring the President's e mail and messages. As she read she became more alert then a smile broke across her face. Her bluff had worked. Sheikh Faisal was on his way to the U.K. That she did not expect but it proved she was right in her thinking. Time to run it past Mike. This could have global ramifications.

She left a message for Mike to call her as soon as possible. He replied almost immediately, "What's up Irene?"

"Something major is happening Mike I have to see you right away."

"Can you come to the office or would you prefer to meet somewhere else?"

"Your office, I'll be there soon as."

That made Mike more than a little worried then he got a call from Liz, "Mike, I thought you should know that Harry's cousin has just arrived, there's live feed on the monitor."

Mike saw James Barnes in the open just outside the entrance to the shed, standing next to his cousin. They seemed to be arguing with James gesticulating wildly then someone came out of the shed holding what looked like a machine gun.

Mike yelled, "Someone get the Superintendent out here right now – run!" The Super arrived breathless.

"Look at this, Mike pointed at the monitor. That's Harry Barnes and his cousin James handling a machine gun in Harry's back yard."

"How are you getting this?"

"Liz, you met her last week, she's one of our detectives and right now is flying a drone at 20,000feet above Harry Barnes's property."

"It's all being recorded right?"

"Oh yes, if we ever needed proof."

As they watched, the three of them walked into the shed with Harry nonchalantly swinging the machine gun back and forth.

Liz said, "I think you've probably seen the crucial part, they'll probably stay inside for quite a while testing out the gun. I'll keep up the surveillance and if anything changes, I'll call you."

"Thanks Liz, that was actually perfect timing, we've got a decision to make now. We'll be in touch."

The Superintendent said, "So what do you think, are you ready to raid the place?"

"Actually, not quite, I'm waiting for one more piece of the puzzle."

When she arrived at the police station Mike was downstairs waiting for her. He took her to his office ignoring all the looks from the detectives sitting at their desks.

"This must be quite important Irene, are you alright?"

"Mike I've been working on this theory for some time. It's something I've kept to myself because it is so far-fetched it is almost unbelievable. I decided to set some traps to bring it to a head and either prove me right or wrong. It turns out I was right. This all revolves around the pharmaceutical company and it all started with my personal investigation. I guess this is the time I have to tell you what that is all about. It is quite personal and I ask you to keep that part of it to yourself. Can you do that for me?"

"Of course, I can, I give you a solemn promise that whatever personal information you tell me stays with me."

"Thanks Mikey, you've no idea what that means to me, I've been holding it in not wanting to tell anyone but it is almost a relief to let it out. This is how it started and that investigation has led to the discovery of what I am about to tell you."

"To start with I am a widow. My husband Ian Wright was a computer expert and head hunted by the pharmaceutical company, I am currently investigating, to work for them. What they offered as an enticement was hard to turn down so we moved here and he was able to introduce systems that saved them millions. As a reward, after they had milked him for what they could, they made him redundant. Ian couldn't handle the rejection and as part of their package they had set up an insurance policy on his life for one hundred million pounds. Ian was so depressed his answer was to step in front of a truck so I could claim the money which is something they never expected. At his funeral not one representative from the pharmaceutical company attended to pay their respects. Right then I made him a solemn promise to avenge his death."

Mike stepped in then, "Irene I am so sorry, what an evil thing to do, you must still be hurting. I have to say I admire how you've been able to rise above that and I completely understand your motivation."

"Thanks Mikey, I appreciate that. Now why I am here. This is important you should take notes because it has global implications. You should perhaps have a witness present as well maybe your Superintendent."

Mike looked a bit alarmed, "Is it really that serious?"

"Yes, it is and having your Superintendent present will also mean you don't have to repeat second hand information. One other thing, for the time being and until this is all resolved I don't want my name mentioned in any report. When it is finalized including the death of my husband then, you can use my name. Are we agreed? This of course includes your Superintendent."

"We are agreed. Now let me get my Superintendent. I'll explain our agreement to him first. Be back as fast as I can."

When Mike left, the office was buzzing. Some people recognized her as the person from Head Office writing a report. Four recognized her as Lara Croft but kept their mouths shut. Mike returned with the Superintendent and there was dead silence. Everyone knew something was going on.

Mike introduced Irene to the Superintendent who put her at ease immediately by saying, "Mike has explained your circumstances and I agree with all your requests.

Now I understand you have something quite important to tell us."

Irene smiled a thank you at Mike and started. "I'll try to make it as short as possible. My background is that I am a Forensic Accountant and an Insolvency Expert. That background makes me a very inquisitive person."

She then went on to explain what she had found out about the President; the shareholders of the pharmaceutical company being related to Osama bin Laden and all payments made to them being transferred to an account in Venezuela. The volatility in that country making it ripe for revolution. Osama's legacy of 29 million dollars to be used for jihad and all the owners of the company were members of Al - Qaeda. She then went on to explain everything she had found out and her measures to bring it all to a head or dismiss it.

"The messages she sent had the desired effect. James Barnes had gone to see his cousin," Mike interrupted.

"Yes, we have it all on tape Liz recorded it all with the drone" Irene continued.

"The message I sent Sheikh Faisal has resulted in something I never anticipated. He is apparently raging and, on his way, here right now."

"I firmly believe that with all the money being transferred to a special account in Venezuela not just from this pharmaceutical company there is a plot to overthrow that government. I've given you all the information I have and my reasons for reaching the conclusions I have. It's up to you now to decide whether to take it forward or decide if I'm stark raving mad. Thanks for listening to me."

The Superintendent spoke first. "Irene, I think you are one of the bravest people I have ever met and I believe everything you have just said and your conclusions."

Mike joined in, "Wow, no wonder you wanted to see me in such a hurry, you've been carrying a big burden but you worked it through, you have great perception, I'm real proud of you. Now the serious stuff starts. We have to work out what to do."

"I think we should take a break and have a bite to eat before we carry on" The Superintendent said, "You two go, I've got to think this through. We'll talk it over when you return."

Sheikh Faisal had left Saudi Arabia almost immediately. He had his own private jet with two pilots and he made sure it was always on the runway ready to go when needed. That policy had paid off time and time again and now was no exception. He was impetuous, bad tempered and used to getting his own way. His wealth had spoiled him and through the years he had very few challengers and those that did more often than not simply disappeared. He was in the air when he sent his message to Thomas Jones Summerville and would be arriving in the U.K. within the next three to four hours.

He was a worried man. What had this Nemesis found out, was it enough to jeopardize his whole operation, he had planned it for years, measures were in place and his men were ready to move, he just had to give the word. He had been to the office before and knew it's layout. He was so arrogant that when he arrived, he just walked straight to the president's office. He was not alone; he had brought twelve "Associates" with him.

The office layout was open plan and all individual offices had glass partitions. The accounts department looked directly into the President's office so Irene had a ringside seat so to speak. She wasn't in her office to watch the entourage sweep in though, she was at the police station. They were all in Arabic clothing, no one was dressed in western suits and ties. The President was a bit startled, not expecting an arrival so soon or the size of the entourage he had brought.

The head of accounts thought she would give Irene a heads up and to get back from her extended lunch as quick as she could. The Sheikh was making quite a show of things ranting away in Arabic. To everyone looking on there was amazement, no one knew the President could speak Arabic and he was not holding back.

Irene and Mike were in the middle of lunch when she got the message from her office. That was quickly followed by a voice message detailing what was going on. She told Mike what was happening and left immediately.

When she got back to her office there wasn't much work going on, everyone was entranced with the spectacle going on in front of them. The Sheikh and the President were still at each other's throats going hammer and tong no holds barred. The twelve "Associates" were wandering about, going into offices, giving all the female staff scathing looks and muttering in Arabic. Irene was observing all of this when two of them swaggered into her office. The way they looked at the girls, laughed at them and made what she interpreted as lewd remarks made them feel very uncomfortable.

"This is not Arabia, get out!"

They didn't expect that and were taken aback.

She repeated in a much louder voice, pointing at the door, "Out!"

They looked at each other, muttered something and left.

Irene looked over at the trainee and said, "Never let bastards like that get away with anything okay!" Then she had another thought, "Do you know how to defend yourself?" The trainee said, "Not really."

"Okay, I teach classes in self-defence, it's a useful skill to have, as demonstrated when you come up against morons like those two who were just in here. Think about it, maybe you and some of your pals would like to learn a thing or two. Let me know."

She smiled at the trainee and even though she had been keeping herself low key she figured that everything was coming to a head now and she wouldn't be here much longer and hopefully neither would the company.

The others in the office were looking at her in a new light and reaching their own conclusions. Several of them had formed a group and were whispering to each other. Finally, they broke up and approached Irene, "Did you mean what you said to Fiona, indicating the trainee?" Irene smiled at them,

"Surprised, are you?"

She was copying Yoda's use of the English language in Star Wars. "Frankly yes and if you mean it, we'd like to be included."

"Good, are you coming as well Fiona?"

"Definitely and I'll bring some of my friends."

"First class will be tomorrow at seven p.m. Wear casual clothes and you will be exercising in bare feet. I'll send the address to your computer screens."

The "Associates" were still milling about making a general nuisance of themselves. The two that Irene had confronted were glowering at her through the glass partition.

The verbal fighting between the President and the Sheikh had died down but there was clearly hostility in the air. The Sheikh said, "I have to know who Nemesis is, why can't you find out?"

"We have tried, even hired outside help but he is too clever, he just can't be traced. Why did you bring all these men with you?"

"I have found it beneficial in the past to have men who can be particularly persuasive if needed."

"What on earth are you talking about, this is not Saudi Arabia. You don't torture people here."

"Get me a suspect and these men will extract the information I want."

"Are you mad? We don't do that sort of thing in the U.K."

"Alright, money talks, it always does. I'll offer a reward for information leading to this person called Nemesis."

"No one has heard of him except the people he sent messages to."

"In my experience, someone knows. I need to know; my plans could be in jeopardy."

"What plans?"

"That's something you don't need to know anything about."

"I'm going to offer a reward of five million pounds for information leading to the discovery of who Nemesis is."

"That is insane!"

"You wait and see. That amount will produce results."

Liz called Mike who answered right away, "There's a lot of activity at Harry's place, vans are starting to arrive and some crates are being carried out of the shed. Looks like he might be ready to make another shipment."

"This might be the time to stop him in his tracks. Keep sending pictures I'm going to organise a wee visiting party."

He went into the Superintendent's office, "Time to raid Harry's place, I'm getting armed response to come along as well."

"Anything you need Mike just ask."

Mike went into the office, "Gather around everyone, the time is nigh. We're going to visit Harry and I'm taking "Armed Response" with us so put your jackets on, you know the way, we'll keep in touch as we go, Liz has spotted increased activity as you can see from the monitor so hopefully, we can now put a stop to his little enterprise. Let's go."

Mike had time to send Irene a quick message – activity at Harry's, on our way to close him down.

Irene read the message and held her breath. She made a quick check to see if cousin James was in the building, then sent Mike a message – James is here.

Mike was communicating with everyone as they approached Harry's house, armed police in first, remember these people are making machine guns. The two police vans roared up the driveway around to the back where the vans had been loaded and piled out shouting, "Armed Police hands in the air!"

The men standing around the vans were in shock at the sudden intrusion and obediently put their hands in the air. There was a lot of shouting then a burst of machine gun fire from the shed. One policeman went down then everyone returned fire. The shooter collapsed in a hail of bullets. The police rushed the shed and shortly after a voice shouted, "All clear!"

Mike ran over to the policeman who had been shot. He was groaning but alive, his bulletproof jacket had saved him. His colleagues quickly surrounded him and gave him first aid. The sergeant in charge turned to Mike, "He was lucky, it's not superficial but serious enough for hospital treatment. He should be fine. Mike then went over to the shed where police were checking over the shooter for identification." He took one look at him and said, "That's Harry Barnes the man behind this operation."

He then went over to the vans and told his men to unload them. It was the same as the previous shipment they had intercepted. Although this time there were slightly more, the cases held 200 sub machine guns. Jubilation all around tempered by the shooting of the police officer. Mike knew Liz was up there watching everything that was going on and even though he couldn't see the drone, looked up, gave a smile and a thumbs up. Next, he called his Superintendent and brought him up to date. His concern was for the policeman who had been shot but Mike reassured him he would be fine and he would be back in the office later on to give him all the details.

He then sent a message to Irene filling her in and that Harry had sneakily opened fire on the police from inside the shed, injured a policeman but paid the ultimate price for his stupidity. We've got enough to arrest James and I'll be doing that as soon as I get back. There might be complications with the Sheikh being there, would you think about that and I'll phone you before I go to your office to arrest him.

Mike then went on to record what was in the shed and call in a team to remove everything and left his detectives to take statements and headed back to his office to get some backup then off to the pharmaceutical company to arrest one James Barnes before he did a disappearing act.

The Superintendent was waiting for him when he reported in, "Huge congratulations Mike, 200 machine guns and Harry Barnes sealed his own fate well done."

"Thanks, now I'm off to arrest his cousin James who showed Harry how to make them. Incidentally there might be a problem on the horizon or more immediately, remember when Irene was here and she explained her theory, well Sheikh Faisal is a very angry man at the anonymous message Irene sent him and flew over here to try and find out who sent it. He's just arrived with what he calls twelve "Associates". I haven't had a chance to talk to her yet but I'm sure there is trouble ahead."

"Mike we could offer her protection."

That got a laugh and he explained that Irene has a black belt in karate and teaches it. "I've seen her in action, in fact she saved me from a severe beating by four criminals sent by Harry Barnes to, as it were 'Sort me out'. No, I think she can look after herself and I pity anyone who messes with her. By the way are you any further forward with what to do with Irene's theory?"

"Yes, I've run it past the chief Constable who has been in touch with the Home Office and the Foreign Secretary."

"Good, they've now got a heads up on what is about to happen and I'm pretty well convinced that with the Sheikh's sudden arrival it's not too far off."

"We'll, I've got some arresting to do so I'd better be off in case our boy decides to do a runner when he finds out about his cousin."

He quickly messaged Irene; I'll be there in about ten minutes any thoughts?

She replied right away, be careful, the Sheikh's "Associates" are nothing but thugs, I've already had a run in with two of them who were leering at one of the young trainees. I had to remind them this is not Saudi Arabia. I'll hang about in case you need back up. His reply was one word – Thanks.

He had four detectives with him when he pulled up in front of the Pharmaceutical Company. They all went to reception together and identified themselves. Mike asked to be escorted to where James Barnes was working without informing him.

As they approached the lab Mike could see Irene lurking about in the background. James Barnes was startled at the police presence. Mike told him he was under arrest for illegal activities. He immediately protested his innocence and demanded his boss was present. He had to bluff his way through it although he had a pretty good idea what it was all about. He had the thought that he would have to warn Harry.

He refused to move until his boss was there. He declared that his boss was the President Thomas Jones Summerville. The President was not accepting any phone calls so another lab technician ran upstairs to verbally tell him that James Barnes was being arrested and wanted him present.

The Sheikh went berserk, "What the hell is going on here!" The President shouted back,

"I have no idea!"

They were both agitated and as the President stormed out of his office the Sheikh was right behind him. His "Associates" perked up and looked at each other undecided then with a nod from the Sheikh followed the two of them down to the lab.

Mike saw them all coming and thought, there's going to be trouble here. The President marched up to Mike and shouted, "Who the hell are you and what's the problem?"

Mike replied in a low and level voice, "The name is O'Neil, Inspector Mike O'Neil and I am here to arrest your lab technician James Barnes for using your facilities for illegal activities and conspiring with others to illegally manufacture weapons for sale to the criminal underworld."

"What! James are you guilty or what's happening here?"

"Not guilty and I don't know what he's on about?"

The Sheikh was hovering threateningly behind the President supported by his "Associates".

Mike looked at James and said, "We can do this one of two ways James, you can come with us voluntarily or you can be cuffed and forcibly removed. What's it to be?"

The Sheikh decided to intervene and moved in front of the lab technician with his "Associates" backing him up.

Mike then said, "James, you have a big decision to make right now, don't mess it up." He then turned to Sheikh Faisal. "This is not a third world country, it is not Saudi Arabia, it is the United Kingdom. Do not openly threaten an officer of the law. If you don't want an international incident and be banned from ever entering this country again, step aside."

The President said something in Arabic to the Sheikh who glowered at Mike but moved aside. Mike then nodded his head at James who shrugged his shoulders in resignation and walked out of the office surrounded by the detectives.

Back in the President's office, the Sheikh was once again shouting and gesticulating wildly, "What kind of company are you running here? Is this man the police just took away really manufacturing guns? Is this place implicated in any way? Interpol, special audits, production problems, and who is Nemesis? What I am going to announce right away is a reward of five million pounds to anyone who can give me information revealing the identity of this man who calls himself Nemesis. I want notices posted immediately and letters sent to all employees… today!"

The President called his secretary and issued the necessary instructions. He privately wished the Sheikh would leave faster than he had arrived. His phone rang and he contemplated not answering it, then his secretary picked it up, shook her head and looked through the glass partition. The President had been watching her and groaned, from her reaction he knew it was not good news.

Irene had been busy sending instructions to the robots, adding ingredients to the formula for the next batch of pain relief medicine. The lab technicians were on the ball this time but not before the robots had made ten thousand capsules. She smiled, the Sheikh won't be too happy with that and wondered what she could do next to liven up his day. She was constantly monitoring all messages and e mails coming from the President and saw the proclamation about to be posted - Sheikh Faisal has authorized a reward of five million pounds for information leading to the unmasking of the man calling himself "Nemesis". She found it slightly amusing that he would automatically think it was a man. Best to keep it that way she thought. With a reward like that she would have to be very careful with every move she made.

She sent a message to Mike – Sheikh Faisal has just issued a reward of five million pounds for information leading to the identity of "Nemesis".

The notices had been posted and the office was abuzz with speculation. Most had never heard of Nemesis and wondered what it was all about. There was hardly any work being done in the offices. All the talk was about the arrest of James Barnes and a five-million-pound reward to reveal who Nemesis was. Irene was fielding questions trying to be as vague as possible and not bring any attention to herself.

Furious discussions were going on in the President's office, more screaming matches than discussions, "I don't know and your five million pounds is just going to have cranks coming forward with wild ideas, wasting time and a lot of unnecessary investigations"

"We will see, you just might be surprised."

James Barnes had been charged and put in a cell. Asked if he wanted to call a solicitor his answer was no but he wanted to call his cousin. Mike debated what to tell him and, in the end, decided to tell him the truth, "James, your cousin Harry was killed this morning in a shootout with the police. He had manufactured 200 sub machine guns and was moving them to the criminal fraternity when we interrupted the shipment. He decided to take a stand and shot one of our police officers from the cover of the shed he made the guns in. With that one act he didn't have a chance.

You've got another choice here James. We know you manufactured guns in the pharmaceutical lab and trained your cousin how to make them as well. No use denying it we have you on video. The smart thing to do here is just confess. It will stand you in good stead with the judge. You don't have long to decide, you'll be going before the court first thing in the morning. I'm here if you want to talk.

Mike then called a meeting with his team, "Did everything get cleared out of the shed?" he asked.

"Yes, answered one of the detectives and there's a bonus. Harry left a list of his contacts and who ordered what and the price. Do you know Harry was charging £2,950 for each machine gun. A piece of plastic moulded on a 3D Printer, who'd have thought it."

"Well done everyone, we've just stopped a major arms manufacturing business. We'll now wait and see what James is going to do."

"We've got another surfacing problem. The largest shareholder of the pharmaceutical company that James Barnes worked for has just arrived in the U.K. with twelve "Associates" on a mission. He is a nasty bit of work and his so called "Associates" are nothing but thugs. When we arrested James Barnes, the Sheikh tried to prevent it by openly placing himself and his Associates in front of him. I had to remind him he was in the U.K. and if he didn't want an international incident he had to step aside. So, we have a man who is an arrogant multimillionaire, has his own plane and used to getting his own way. He is here for a purpose, so keep all of that in mind. There's more to come.

Sheikh Faisal was doing his dinger, he could see problems building up for his Venezuelan Operation, complicated now by the revelation of what James Barnes had been up to and the involvement of Nemesis. He had once again lost his cool and was blaming the President for everything. For his part, Thomas Jones Summerville was also raging. He had no idea James Barnes was illegally making guns and using company equipment to do it. He knew there was going to be a massive police investigation and he was worried at what this "Nemesis" might reveal. Obviously, the Sheikh was so worried he flew here to try and get to the bottom of it but he was also hiding something, other plans that could be put in jeopardy, important enough to offer a five-million-pound reward for information, what in hell was going on.

The Sheikh was now talking to his "Associates" who were listening intently to his instructions then strode out of the President's office with a clear purpose.

They had been instructed to do the only thing they knew best. Fear, intimidation and threats – they had to find Nemesis. The only thing they hadn't taken into account, because it was alien to their way of thinking, they just couldn't do anything they wanted. They were not in Saudi Arabia they were in the U.K.

All the Associates could speak English, they separated and went in pairs to each floor, department by department. Soon the complaints came pouring in. Intimidation and threats. There was one case of physical violence when one male worker who told the Associates to "Get stuffed!" and was shoved against a wall. Human Resources department was flooded with complaints. The President was informed and went ballistic. The Sheikh ignored him and shouted, "I need results!"

Irene was in her office with five others when two Associates swaggered in. They singled out the young trainee and started shouting and threatening her. Irene intervened, went over and told them to get out. They made the mistake of demeaning all women as lesser humans and shoved her aside... big mistake... the first Associate who had shoved her had his hand twisted around and his arm forced up and twisted out of its socket, as he shrieked in pain and doubled up, Irene lifted her knee, smashed it into his chin then punched him squarely in the face, breaking his nose and smashing several of his teeth before he fell unconscious to the floor.

The second Associate yelled in Arabic and produced a wicked looking dagger from the folds of his cloak. Several of the women screamed but Irene faced him and said, "You shouldn't have done that."

Because the offices were open plan and glass partitioned, everyone could see what was going on including the President and the Sheikh. The President shouted,

"What the hell!" and rushed out of his office closely followed by the Sheikh.

Irene was in complete control and crouched slightly facing the swirling dagger. As the Arab made what he thought was a dazzling move Irene stepped in close and stiffed him in the throat with her right hand, fingers rigid and close together. The Associate dropped his dagger, grabbed his throat and started choking. It was then that Irene turned sideways and lashed out with her right foot connecting with his knee joint. As he went down, she gave him a quick chop to the back of his neck. He hit the floor completely unconscious.

The Sheikh was in the office by this time and Irene turned to face him expecting another assault. She crouched and gestured with her hands with a movement that said," Come on". She was sure he was going for it when the President shouted in Arabic, "Stop it!"

Irene took the initiative, "Who the hell do you think you are!"

This was directed at the Sheikh then she said to the President, "I'm calling the police, these two, indicating the Associates on the floor are going to be charged with attempted murder and this one, nodding at the Sheikh, seems to be in charge and will also be charged. They will all be staying in this country for a long time. I hope the police decide to put them in the cells."

The President and the Sheikh were dumbfounded at the turn of events. Irene turned to her workmates, smiled and said, "Remember, the first lesson is tomorrow night."

Mike was on his way to the cells. James Barnes had requested a meeting. He was almost at the cells when his phone rang loudly and a member of his team was running down the corridor shouting, "Mike! Mike!"

He stopped and turned around. The detective was breathless as he told him what had happened at the pharmaceutical company, his phone was still ringing and he could see it was Irene.

"What's happened, are you alright?"

"Yes, but there are two so called "Associates" who aren't. One pulled a knife on me and they are on the way to hospital right now. The Sheikh ordered his men to play rough with the staff to find out who Nemesis is. I'm not telling you your job Mike but the two on their way to hospital should be charged with attempted murder along with the Sheikh and by the way he flew over here in his private jet and I wouldn't put it past him if he made a break for it to try and leave the country."

"I'll be there as fast as I can"

He then made phone calls to make sure the Sheikh's plane was grounded and that he and his men were not allowed to leave the country. It was also important that he spoke to James Barnes. His cell was a short distance away and he ran to it. James was waiting for him, "Well James have you made a decision?"

"I have, can we make a deal?"

"What do you have to offer?"

"I can give you details of how I made the guns and how Harry set up his manufacturing site."

"Anything else? Because if that's it, all you can do is throw yourself at the mercy of the judge. I'll get a stenographer to take your statement."

He then made a beeline for the front of the building where a car was waiting to speed him to the pharmaceutical company.

Irene was right. The Sheikh and his entourage had slipped out the back door and were piling into two range rovers. The old adage, to be forewarned certainly paid off. As they tried to leave, four police cars, sirens blaring, came screeching to a halt and blocked the range rover's escape. It was an armed response unit and they promptly took charge. The Sheikh and his Associates were arrested and handcuffed. A paddy wagon pulled up and they were unceremoniously thrown in the back and driven off to a specialist police station used for serious crimes.

Three police cars sped up to the company building, Mike leapt out of the lead car and raced into the building. The ambulance crew were just taking out the two "Associates", he asked.

"How are they?"

"They'll survive, but need surgery"

He went upstairs to the President's office where several police were taking statements and showing a lot of interest in Irene. Mike went up to them and said, "Ok, boys, I'll take over from here."

6.

REVOLUTION

Irene looked at him and said, "Am I glad to see you. It's all come to a head now. I think the President is as confused as everyone else. Basically, the Sheikh and his relatives own this company, and I'm sure that if we look closer into the affiliated pharmaceutical companies, we'll find they are also owned by the Sheikh. I firmly believe all the profits, by way of bonuses and special dividends, find their way to fund a revolution in Venezuela. I think the Sheikh is behind it, and it will be in turmoil with him in jail. Mind you, expect international repercussions because he is well-connected with the Royal Family, and he is filthy rich. I wouldn't be surprised if political circles are involved already.

"Right, have you made your statement to the police?"

"Yes, but I'm sure they wanted to question me some more."

"Don't worry about that; I'll have a word. Now we have to get to the station; the chief needs to have a talk because we are going to a meeting with the Home Office and the

Foreign Secretary. Depending on the outcome, they've reserved a spot for talks at the United Nations."

Irene looked shocked and said, "I just wanted justice for Ian."

Mike's phone started ringing loudly with constant bursts of the ringtone. He looked at Irene, "That's the boss. It means urgent; we have to get to the office, and he ushered her to the car out front. As it sped off, Irene said, "There's a lot more going on. Do you want me to tell you now or wait till we get to your office?"

"Tell me now."

I've been monitoring the President's messages and e-mails. He's been telling his friends to sell their shares in the pharmaceutical company and invest the money in a company listed on the international stock market. Claims it is rock bottom right now but will soar very shortly. He added that this is a major tip, and he can't reveal his sources; otherwise, he could go to jail for a very long time if the authorities find out.

It would appear that Mr Thomas Jones Summerville has decided to look after number one, but for a supposedly intelligent man, he has made a very stupid mistake by admitting on paper that what he is doing is illegal; it's basically called insider trading. The next part you are not going to believe. I found this by going into the dark web, and I'm not sure if I should reveal that to a lot of people.

The company he is recommending is called "Rock Investments". It apparently invests in mining companies, especially those start-ups seeking materials to supply the manufacture of batteries used in electric cars. Everyone wants to pile into that. The company was only established two months ago, and already, because of heavy advertising and the likes of Thomas Jones Summerville, it has a fund value of close to nine hundred million pounds and is starting to pay its shareholders dividends. The thing is, it hasn't invested any money in any mining company or anything else. So, you might ask, how are they able to pay dividends? Have you ever heard of a Pyramid Scheme? Well, this is one: it is illegal, and people are enticed into investing with the promise of great rewards; only the new money going into the fund is used to pay whatever dividends the fund manager decides, and if you can show great dividends, you'll get more investors but it is not sustainable, and it will eventually fail.

The main purpose of setting up this fund, however, is to siphon off money for other purposes. By the way, you can be charged and face a heavy fine or imprisonment if convicted of operating a pyramid scheme.

Now, this next bit is going to blow your mind.

"Rock Investments" is owned by none other than Sheikh Faisal's brother, Mohammed Ali. Faisal.

He is a devout Jihadist and extreme follower of Osama bin Laden's beliefs, as well as being a distant relative. He also has a home in Venezuela, and I'm convinced he is the one making all the plans for the revolution. All the money from the dividends, etc., paid out by the pharmaceutical companies, as well as the money from "Rock Investments" is going towards the revolution. One other thing. During the ten years the President lived in Saudi Arabia, he was paid millions by Sheikh Faisal to set up a pharmaceutical company here in the U.K. No one knows about that money, and it is sitting in a secret bank account in Saudi Arabia. Finally, it is not officially known or advertised, but in the company, records registered for "Rock Investments" the Chief Financial Officer is listed as Thomas Jones Summerville. This man is up to his eyeballs in skulduggery.

"My God! How on earth did you dig up all this information?"

"That's what I do, Mike."

"This is going to have major repercussions; well done."

When they arrived at the police station, official government limousines were lined up with drivers standing beside them. The downstairs was full of people, and Mike recognized several newspaper reporters. He turned to Irene and said,

"Whatever's going on, do not say one word to any of the reporters. We go inside and straight up to the chief's office."

As they went into the building, several of his team emerged from the crowd and surrounded them, fending off anyone who approached them. Mike asked what was going on and was told, "Its two things: thanking us for discovering and stopping gun manufacturing and Sheikh Faisal and the pharmaceutical company. The Deputy Home Office Minister is here; they're putting the screws on the Chief for arresting the Sheikh and causing an international incident. The Superintendent is in there as well."

"Thanks, boys. Don't go away; I just might need you."

Mike walked into the Chief's office with Irene, and the relief on his face when he saw them was palpable, "Afternoon, Chief, Superintendent, I've got a verbal report to give, and I'll follow that up with a written statement."

He didn't let the Home Office minister get a word in. He tried, but Mike could see he was a man full of his own importance trying to Lord it over the Chief.

"I've arrested Sheikh Faisal for wilfully instructing his men to terrorize employees of the pharmaceutical company, causing bodily harm to one employee, inflicting harm on another by physically attacking her, and the attempted murder of another by producing a concealed weapon, namely an illegal knife all on the instructions of Sheikh Faisal. I have arrested the two so called "Associates" who carried out the attack and the person behind it who verbally gave the instructions, one Sheikh Faisal. They are being charged with attempted murder".

Mike had successfully pre-empted the Home Office Minister from making any protestations. He did try, however, by demanding the immediate release of the Sheikh.

"Over my dead body! On what grounds, even if you know he has caused an international incident, release him! Don't you know the law? He has been arrested, and when he appears before the court, I'll be asking the judge to keep him in custody until his trial. Now, I suggest you leave this office and rethink your position. I did not expect incompetence at this level of government."

The Deputy Home Office Minister slammed the door behind him as he left, shouting,

"You'll hear about this!"

The chief looked at Mike and said, "Well done, I back you 100%."

The Superintendent added, "Well-spoken I'm right behind you as well. Interestingly, we have a meeting with the Home Office Minister within the next half hour."

"Before we go there, you should hear this."

Mike then went over what Irene had just told him. She filled in the details as he went along, and when he finished, he said, "Because of what's involved, the impending overthrow of a government, I think the Foreign Secretary should be at that meeting as well; hell, let's not stop there. We should get the Prime Minister involved as well. "Everyone smiled, and then the Chief said, "That's not such a daft idea. Irene, can you back up what you have discovered?"

"Every bit of it. I can give you printouts, and I've already told you the bank account details where payments from employees of the pharmaceutical company are being sent. Interpol should be able to delve deeper into that, and I can give them details of other accounts. There is no doubt in my mind that Osama bin Laden's Acolytes are planning a revolution in Venezuela."

The Superintendent looked at Irene, "I've said this before, and I'll say it again, you are a very brave woman. What you have done is quite remarkable. Now I've heard rumours. Is it true you disabled two of the Sheikh's so called "Associates"? Irene did not elaborate but simply said, "I have a black belt, fifth Dan, in karate."

"Good for you. Now, the way this story is unfolding, I would expect you will be in great demand in political circles, both domestic and International. Are you OK with that?"

"No problem, people like this have to be stopped. I started off seeking revenge for my husband who killed himself because of the avarice of this pharmaceutical company, and I just stumbled into this web of intrigue."

"I am truly sorry for your loss, Irene. We will do our best to right that wrong."

The chief said, "Mike, we have a lot of preparations to do and phone calls to make, so while we put a case together, can one of your team look after Irene?"

Remembering that Irene got on with Liz, the drone pilot, he asked her if that would be okay.

"Fine by me."

"You'll have to use your own judgment at what you tell her, and I'm sure the rest of the team will be curious as well. Any questions, more recollections, points you think should be raised, we are right here."

He then took her out to Liz and said, "You remember Irene? Can you look after her for a while? We have a lot to discuss."

"I'll be delighted, Mike."

The rest of the team were all smiles and also full of curiosity. Especially four detectives who were making up their minds to ask her about "Lara Croft" and who she really was, from being a special adviser to the chief constable to working at the pharmaceutical company to beating the hell out of two Saudi Arabian thugs and now involved in high-level discussions. The whole office was buzzing, especially after Mike had thrown out the Deputy Home Office Minister.

They shook hands, hesitated for a minute, and then gave each other a hug. "Nice to see you again," Irene said to Liz.

"Likewise," came the reply.

Slowly, the other detectives wandered over to join in the conversation. Irene recognized that rather than be pumped with questions. She should just come clean and not tell them everything but enough to satisfy their curiosity.

She started by saying, "I've got a funny feeling we're going to be working together for a while, and I know you are all wondering who the devil I am, so I'm going to tell you. Mike told me to use my own discretion. The only thing I ask is that you keep it to yourselves. I don't want to read about myself in the papers; I trust you, okay?"

There was a chorus of "Okay, you can trust us."

Irene said, "Good, so here we go."

"My name is Irene Wright. I'm a widow, and my husband killed himself because of this pharmaceutical company's greed. He was an I.T. expert and had saved the company he worked for tens of thousands of pounds, so he was headhunted by this pharmaceutical company with an offer he couldn't refuse. We moved here, and in turn, he saved this company hundreds of thousands with his programming skills; then, when they couldn't get any more out of him, they made him redundant and claimed it was a restructuring. He couldn't handle that and decided to kill himself. I vowed to avenge his death, so I got a job in the accounts department using my maiden name to try and make them pay.

I am a forensic accountant and an insolvency expert, and by the way, I also have a black belt, fifth Dan, in karate. During my investigations into the company, I discovered the gun manufacturing business, and now we have this carry-on with Sheikh Faisal. That has global ramifications, and I don't think I should talk about it just now. That's what the boys are doing.

So that's the story so far, and by the way, I teach classes in self-defence. Several of the women in the pharmaceutical company have signed up, so if anyone is interested, just let me know."

Liz said, "I'm sure I speak for everyone here, Irene; you've had a difficult time, so sorry for your loss, and if we can do anything, anything, we are here for you."

There was a spontaneous clapping of hands that made Mike and everyone in the office look up. Mike could see Irene had won them over and smiled; she was now part of the team.

Mohammed Ali Faisal was not a happy man. Years of planning were starting to go down the Swanee. He and his brother had spent years planning this, the biggest gamble of their lives; bribes, promises, coercion, blackmail, all went into it, and they were on the verge, but something had gone wrong in the U.K. Now Interpol was interfering. What the hell had his brother done? He couldn't reach him, couldn't talk to him, and had to ask others involved in the coup where he was and what had happened.

The country was ripe for revolution. It was engulfed in crime, hyperinflation, and political corruption. Millions had already left the country, and the brothers reasoned it wouldn't take much to create a general uprising. They didn't have any feelings of goodwill for the Venezuelans had no lofty ideals to set them free for a better life; all they were interested in was getting their hands on the nation's oil. The oil sands alone had deposits equal to the world reserves of conventional oil. It was greed, pure greed that motivated them.

He finally got the news he was waiting for, and it wasn't what he was expecting. His brother was in jail for attempted murder. How the hell did that happen? Then, the details followed. If this coup was to succeed, he needed his brother. Who in the hell was this Nemesis?

He had to take care of him and get his brother out of jail. He sent messages back: "Money is no problem, repeat – no problem, get my brother out of jail and eliminate this Nemesis! - Repeat money is no problem; I expect results!"

Increased pressure was being put on the government to release Sheikh Faisal from the Saudi Arabian Government to the team of high-priced lawyers his brother had hired.

Mike called Irene into the office. Not only had Mike, the Superintendent, and the Chief of police, they had now been joined by the Crown Prosecution Services. They were the people who decided if a case should go to court and what the charges were after the police had investigated it. The C.P.S. makes its decisions independently of the police and government. They advise the police, prepare the case, and present it to the court.

Irene was introduced and immediately congratulated on uncovering the international web of intrigue and the intended coup in Venezuela. As far as Sheikh Faisal and his two Associates were concerned, it was a case of self-defence, and with the introduction of a hidden dagger, it was definitely a case of attempted murder by the two Associates. They had a problem with charging Sheikh Faisal.

"All the Associates, who could speak perfect English, only spoke in Arabic and denied the Sheikh had instructed them to be heavy-handed with the pharmaceutical staff in trying to find out who "Nemesis" was. They were just acting as they would in Saudi Arabia and didn't realize their interrogation methods were not acceptable in the U.K. The trouble is, we only have hearsay evidence of any instructions from the Sheikh. None of them verified any instructions were given. No one actually heard him, and all that was seen was the Sheikh talking to his men. We would be ripped apart if we presented this as evidence in court.

We might know the truth, but I'm sure these so-called Associates all know if they say one word against the Sheikh, they and their families would pay the price. We all know they have no regard for human life. I'm afraid we cannot charge the Sheikh, even though we might know he is guilty."

"On top of all that, you have no idea the amount of pressure Saudi Arabia has heaped on our government to release the Sheikh. Mind you, that would have no bearing on whether we decide to pursue a case or not. This is what I think is going to happen. The two Associates who attacked you will definitely be charged with attempted murder. We don't have enough to charge the Sheikh. His lawyers will try to make some kind of deal to get the two associates off. We will ask for the immediate expulsion of the other ten Associates. I'm afraid that's the best we can do. At least you have the satisfaction of having put two of them out of action for some time. By the way, it's not necessary for you to go to court. We've scheduled that for tomorrow at eleven a.m."

Irene thanked them for all they had done to prosecute the Sheikh but understood their position. Once the C.P.S. had left, Irene said, "Remember that the Sheikh is a majority shareholder in the pharmaceutical company. He and his cousins own the business, and now we've discovered that the President, Thomas Jones Summerville, is the chief financial officer of 'Rock Investments', set up by the brother Mohammed Ali Faisal, with investments now approaching one billion pounds. It would be interesting to know if the Sheikh has any knowledge of this arrangement with his brother. Is there any trust within that family? I don't know, and we'll have to wait and see what the Sheikh does when he is released from jail."

Mike followed that with, "In the meantime, we have arranged a meeting with the Home Office Secretary, Foreign Office Secretary, Interpol, and because of the implications of a coup in Venezuela, a senior member of the United Nations. That is taking place in two hours in Downing Street."

Irene shook her head, "I can't believe how fast things have moved from seeking justice for my husband to an impending coup in Venezuela and a high-powered meeting in Downing Street, which I presume the Prime Minister will be attending."

Mike confirmed that with a nod.

The Chief Constable said, "Right, a lot of preparation to do in two hours; we'd better get started."

The meeting in Downing Street was not what you would say, a low-key affair. Irene met people she had only seen on television; only this time, she was the centre of attention.

She was congratulated several times on uncovering the plot to overthrow the Venezuelan government and how it was being funded. The U.N. representative couldn't quite believe the clandestine way the brothers Faisal were raising and transferring funds without any suspicion falling on them.

"This is a real danger facing not only Venezuela but the world if the oil deposits fall into the hands of these brothers. It is bad enough how Vladimir Putin's 'Military Exercise' against Ukraine has affected world stability and oil prices, but if these two get their way, there is no telling how it will turn out."

The representative from Interpol said, "You have done a remarkable investigation, Mrs Wright, and we have thoroughly checked your work. There is no question about it; they almost got away with it, and without your vigilance, we would be witnessing another civil war. That country is so mismanaged with rampant corruption we have to do our best to intervene and prevent bloodshed on a massive scale. We, along with the U.N. and your Prime Minister, have advised the Venezuelan Government of an impending insurrection. As we speak, they are taking measures to prevent that happening and find those responsible. Would you be able to spend some time with us to go over the details of how you discovered what was happening? It's perhaps premature of me to say this, but Interpol would welcome you with open arms if you ever decide to leave your current employment."

"That's very flattering of you, and yes, I'd be more than happy to go over how I arrived at my findings with you."

The Prime Minister added, "You've done a remarkable job, and as a nation, we are very proud of you. If there is anything we can ever do for you, you only have to ask."

Irene smiled, said thank you, and looking the Prime Minister right in the eye, said, "I'm sure I'll think of something."

As the meeting broke up, Mike said to Irene, "Do you want me with you when you talk to Interpol?"

"Yes, I think that is probably a good idea."

The next day, the C.P.S. was in court proceeding with the action against Sheikh Faisal and his two associates. The courtroom was packed. Many Arab countries were present to give their support to the accused. What happened next was extraordinary. As the court convened, the lead counsel for the Sheikh and his associates stood up and said, "Your honour, I wish to make a statement."

He got the nod to go ahead. The lawyer representing C. P. S. John Brown perked up at that because, normally, any statement presented to the court is discussed with the opposition first.

"The Sheikh has accepted that his men overstepped the boundaries and created a state of fear and anxiety in the workforce of the pharmaceutical company. In particular, two of his men were involved in an altercation with an employee. They came off worse as a result and are still recuperating in hospital. At no time did the Sheikh Issue instructions for his men to act in an aggressive manner towards employees of the company."

At that point, John Brown stood up and interjected, "Your Honour, we haven't even set out our case or, indeed has the Court proclaimed what the purpose of this action is all about, and we have the defence lawyer reading straight from Grimm's 'Fairy Tales'."

The Judge said, "Mr Ashbury, I have given you some leeway, but this does not appear to be a statement. You either make that statement or sit down, and we proceed with the case against your client."

Suitably chastised, Mr Ashbury apologized and continued. "The Sheikh recognizes that errors of judgment were made and would like to pay compensation to the employees for their actions. At the same time, we propose a suitable fine is levied against these two associates, and they are repatriated to their home country to serve any sentence meted out by their legal system, and all charges against the Sheikh are dropped."

John Brown leaped to his feet, "Your Honour! Was all he got out?"

The Judge's face was red with anger, "Mr Ashbury! You should know better. These are all matters that should have been discussed with the police before you came to court, and any charges adjusted accordingly. You are wasting court time! Mr Brown, now that we are here and to avoid a long delay for the next available court time, how would you like to proceed?"

John Brown already knew he couldn't successfully charge the Sheikh, and he reasoned it would probably be beneficial to get the two Associates deported ... but they were going to have to pay for it. It's best to get it over and done with right now. He held the high card. He knew the Sheikh wanted out of jail to pursue his Venezuelan interests, but the Sheikh didn't know that.

"Ok, you're Honour, let's get it sorted right now. I'll agree to release the Sheikh and his two Associates on condition that they, along with the other ten Associates he brought with him, are deported with the restriction that they are never allowed to return. A suitable compensation is agreed for the pharmaceutical company employees and a fine for all the trouble and wasted time. We agree on an amount right now, and it is paid before they are released."

The Judge said, "That seems like the sensible solution, Mr Ashbury, do you agree?"

"Yes, you're Honour, just give me a minute to confer with my client."

It was longer than a minute, and they were arguing violently before Mr Ashbury broke away and said, "We are prepared to offer a total of Fifty million pounds your Honour."

The judge looked at John Brown, eyebrows raised wanting a response.

He was going to pay for his freedom, which he knew the Sheikh desperately wanted, and his deceit thought the prosecutor and replied, "That will do for the compensation to all employees, now the rest, and think carefully before you answer. Don't take long; I and the court have other things to do; we've wasted enough time as it is."

More arguing, then Mr Ashbury said, "We will pay a total of one hundred million pounds."

The judge looked at John Brown, eyebrows raised once again.

"Make it two hundred million pounds, and we have a deal."

Everyone in the courtroom gasped, but John Brown just stared at the Sheikh, almost daring him to refuse the payment. The Sheikh was in a state of, what you might say, near apoplexy, but he knew he had to get out and get in touch with his brother and finish the Venezuelan project. His final thought was, *that damned Nemesis!*

As the arresting officer, Mike was in court in case he was needed. He just smiled and thought, good for you, John.

It was agreed, and John Brown said he would draw up the release papers with the conditions imposed. The Judge said he would witness them, and all that was needed was the transfer of two hundred million pounds, and the Sheikh and his Associates would be released.

When Mike got back to the station and told everyone what had happened, there was genuine disbelief. The C.P.S. had realized they couldn't successfully charge the Sheikh and also knew why he wanted his freedom, so they made sure he paid for it. It was an incredible amount of money, and Mike told everyone he was going to work with the C.P.S. to make sure it was fairly distributed. The first thing was to ring fence fifty million pounds for the employees of the pharmaceutical company, with roughly 300 people working there, which equated to around £165K for each employee. Mike reasoned there was a very high probability that the company would shortly no longer exist and the employees would need that money.

Thomas Jones Summerville couldn't quite believe what was happening. In the space of a very short time, the company had gone from a successful operation to one mired in illegal activities, from a V.P. accepting bribes, the illegal manufacture of guns, and an investigation by Interpol, to the main shareholder, Sheikh Faisal being arrested for attempted murder. Where had my quiet existence gone, all my planning for the future? Maybe with the impending release of the Sheikh, it was time to get out.

He had the original bribe money to set up the pharmaceutical company still in a bank in Saudi that no one knew about except the Sheikh. He also had a secret deal with Mohammed, the Sheikh's brother, "Rock Investments". There was a lot of money in there, and it was growing. Yes, maybe it was time to make a move.

Irene decided to go back to work at the pharmaceutical company. She still had some unfinished business there. The President had to pay for the death of her husband. She talked it over with Mike, who was vehemently opposed to the idea. It was too dangerous, but her mind was made up, and there was no way it could be changed.

Her return was met with a mixed reaction. Most welcomed her back with congratulations on taking care of the two "Associates", but she could feel that others, like the management team, looked at her quite differently now. It was time to wrap this up as quickly as possible.

Thomas Jones Summerville could see her return from his office and decided it would be best to have a word with her. He went into her office and apologized for the actions of the Sheik's two "Associates". Irene accepted his apology and said, "You know, the Sheikh and his men treat women quite differently in Saudi Arabia, and that behaviour is just not acceptable in the U.K. I don't think they'll do that again."

The President nodded his head and left her office with all the other people in there chattering away.

7.

RETRIBUTION

The transfer had been made, and the Sheikh and his men were released from prison. They were given forty-eight hours to put their affairs in order before they were deported.

They had barely been released when they charged into the office. No one was more surprised than Thomas Jones Summerville. There were no pleasantries exchanged. The Sheikh started shouting in Arabic, and it took no time for the two of them to be shouting at each other. The Associates were told to sit in the waiting area and wait.

Irene sent Mike a quick message. "Could be trouble brewing here; the Sheikh and his merry men just stormed in, and he and the President are going at it hammer and tong in Arabic. I'll keep you informed."

She then got in touch with Interpol. She'd been given a number to phone if she had an update, and she told them what was happening right now.

"Can you tell me what's happening in Venezuela?"

"Yes, sure can; all hell is breaking out. Mohammed bribed the Mechanised Division but not certain elements of the army, and you could say they are slugging it out right now. He was also in the process of bribing the air force and seemed to be fairly successful in that endeavour. This revolution could actually go either way right now. Keep me posted on developments at your end, and I'll do the same here."

There was basically no work being done in the offices. Everyone was mesmerised by the spectacle taking place in front of them. The Sheikh and the President were now approaching the shoving and pushing stage of their very vociferous argument. If only she could speak Arabic, Irene thought. I'd love to know what they are on about; then she heard one word in English: Nemesis.

Now then, she surmised maybe I should send them both a final message, really send the Sheikh over the edge. She went into the dark web and made sure the messages could not be traced back to her. First, the Sheikh. How's your revolution working out pal? Are you aware of the secret deal your brother made with Thomas? You've only got forty-eight hours! Don't think you got away with it… Justice awaits, Signed: Nemesis.

Next, the President. Cosy deal you made with Mohammed. For that alone, you're going straight to jail. Kiss the good life goodbye. Signed: Nemesis

Irene smiled. She was in a commanding position now, and with the current ultra-high speed of the internet, she should be able to see their reactions from her office. She settled back in her chair and waited.

It didn't take long. Both messages pinged at the same time, both men read them at the same time, and both men went deathly quiet at the same time. Their attitudes changed dramatically. Whatever they were arguing about was forgotten. They both looked at each other suspiciously, then both sat down and started talking.

"So, what deal did you do with my brother?"

"Here's the message I just received. Let me see yours." Irene could see them exchanging telephones and thought, *interesting, very interesting. It seemed that her messages had the effect of bringing them back together, not at all what she had expected.*

The Sheikh said, "I think we're being watched by this person Nemesis."

"I think you're probably right. I brought in specialists when the first messages appeared, trying to trace the origin but to no avail. My question is, where is he getting all his information from? There is basically only you, me and your brother who knows all the details. It must be someone in our organisation who is either "Nemesis" or is feeding a third party with information, and for what purpose? Have you received any blackmail threats? Anyone asking for money?"

"No, I haven't."

"Then what is the purpose? Where is this leading?"

"Maybe we should start looking more closely at the people in the I.T. department."

"We've already done that and found nothing. Perhaps we should do one thing only you and I know about and hope that draws him out."

"OK, let's think about that; in the meantime, I only have forty-eight hours left in this country. We have a lot to sort out before they deport me."

Irene was watching them very closely. Now they were co-conspirators; she could tell they were planning something, but what?

Five new faces appeared in the waiting area. They were dressed in Western clothes, but they were definitely not Western. Swarthy and short, they would definitely not be described as choir boys, more like members of a very nasty underworld gang. Which is exactly what they were. Set up by the ruling body In Saudi Arabia, they were based in London to silence dissidents who spoke out too loudly against their authority. They were also for hire, and right now, it was Mohammed, Sheikh Faisal's brother, who had hired them to help out his brother.

The waiting area was at the far end of the office, and Irene could just see the flurry of activity as the mercenaries arrived. She wondered what was happening; then she saw five men being escorted by the Sheikh's "Associates" into the President's office. One look at them, and her heart skipped a beat. These were no ordinary thugs. She could see at once they were experienced killers.

The President and the Sheikh were not expecting anyone and were as shocked as everyone else at their entrance. The leader bowed his head to the Sheikh and started talking. They were loud, but it was all in Arabic, so she didn't understand a word they said. You didn't have to understand the language to realise this was the heavy mob. One look at them would give you the willies. Arrogant and full of their own importance, they looked around, almost daring anyone to challenge them. Irene knew immediately there was trouble ahead.

"Best to let Mike know," and she phoned rather than send him a message.

"Mike, bad news, five new arrivals have just joined the Sheikh's 'Associates'. They're a different breed, killers to the core. I don't think they were expected, but they are here for a purpose; there's going to be trouble, so be prepared. I'm going to take pictures of them because I have the feeling they didn't just fly in; they are already living here. You might have them on your mug file or whatever you call it."

She used her smartphone and once again marvelled at the advances in technology. Pictures were now every bit as good as expensive cameras and, in some cases, even better. At least now we had a visual record of the Sheikh's men.

Irene could see things were rapidly coming to a head. There was something going on with the arrival of this new contingent. Her contact in Interpol was a Frenchman named Francois, and she gave him a heads up on the latest developments and sent him a copy of the pictures she had just taken. Perhaps they had a "Rogues Gallery" where the latest arrivals could be identified.

"There's one other thing, Francois; Mohammed is part-funding this revolution with money from an investment fund he calls 'Rock Investments'. He created the fund with the help of the President of the pharmaceutical company, Mr Thomas Jones Summerville, who, by the way, is listed as the Chief Financial Officer. It is an illegal Pyramid scheme with funds of hundreds of millions of pounds. I am about to deplete that fund to zero and transfer the money into another account. That will put the wind-up."

"Wait a minute, you can do that?"

"You'd be surprised at what I can do, Francois."

"Actually, no, I don't think I would be surprised, Irene."

"So, what I am going to do right now is transfer the money into an international account that holds billions for world countries until they are needed. That account is so big, with a constant movement of funds, that no one will notice it. The question is what to do with it when this is all over. I'm sure there is a lot of illegal money in there, from money laundering to drug money. These people invested purely out of greed with money gained purely from illegal activities."

"Talking of illegal activities, Irene, I'm sure what you are about to do is illegal."

"What do you want, Francois, to be kept in the dark about what is going on in the world or be part of an operation to put a stop to it?"

"How are you going to do that?"

"Best, you probably don't know. You have enough information to arrest Mohammed and Thomas Jones Summerville. I would suggest you work that out with the powers to be while I take care of making that Fund worthless."

"One final thing, Irene, have you thought any more about joining our organisation?"

"Thinking Francois, thinking. If you want another group meeting or physical evidence, let me know."

It didn't take Irene long to shift the money and make "Rock Investments" worthless. Maybe that would act as a catalyst to find out what was happening.

Mike phoned, followed shortly after by Francois, even though she had just talked to him. Both had files on the five new arrivals. Both advised her to stay well clear of them, and both said they were putting surveillance around the clock on them. She messaged back, looks like things are about to kick off. Mike messaged, "I have an armed team on standby just let me know if they are needed."

Francois messaged Mike and Irene, "Interpol wants a meeting with the previous participants because of the rapidly changing circumstances. Please make arrangements and advise."

There were too many people crammed into the President's office. They were now starting to raise their voices, and there was some pushing and shoving going on. People were starting to move into the hallway rather aimlessly, looking for a purpose. Irene could see it was building and turned to the girls in her office.

"I think you should all leave right now. Get out of the building, try not to draw attention to yourselves and don't alarm anyone. Don't leave en masse, just in ones and twos. Start now."

The Associates and new arrivals now seemed to be a cohesive force, but Irene could see they were waiting for direction. They were almost like caged lions. Most of the girls had left the office without suspicion. Two of the new arrivals were in the President's office, quite blatantly checking over Glock 19s.

Irene sent a quick message to Mike, "The associates and new arrivals have blended and are restless. They have also brought weapons with them. I saw two Glock 19s. I've sent the girls in the office out of the building."

Mike replied immediately, "Get out of the building."

"If I do, you won't know what's going on. It's safe just now; I just don't know why the new arrivals are here. It might be an idea to phone others in the building and get them to quietly leave. No telling what's going to happen."

The frustration was starting to show. The new arrivals, in particular, were marching up and down the corridors, going into offices, kicking desks, then abruptly going out again. One of them walked into Irene's office, stared at her for a long time, and then went up close to her. This was a different breed of man, and she didn't rise to his actions but was prepared to teach him the facts of life if he went too far.

The Sheikh's phone rang. It was a soft mid-eastern tone that surprised Irene. He answered and then started screaming. Irene heard the name Mohammed and presumed it was his brother phoning. She could only imagine he had found out that "Rock Investments" was now bankrupt. He started shouting at Thomas Jones Summerville, who became quite pale. In between the Sheikh's shouting, he repeatedly yelled the name Nemesis. It would appear her actions had the desired effect. She quickly messaged Francois, the shit has hit the fan, arrest

Mohammed before he disappears. She then sent Mike a similar message, adding if you can get Interpol in here to arrest the President and the Sheikh, so much the better. I think they are all ready to take flight. Careful! They are all armed!

She then sat back and waited. Mike must have been prepared and probably sitting in a van outside with Interpol agents. The door burst open, and a flood of police and Interpol agents, all heavily armed, rushed in, pointing their weapons and shouting, "Hands in the air! Hands in the air!"

They outnumbered the Sheikh and his men by at least two to one, and they weren't messing about. They quickly disarmed and handcuffed the Sheikh and his men, leaving a pale and shaking Thomas Jones Summerville to the last.

Before they were taken away, Irene looked at Francois and Mike. A word with them first, please. They both nodded, and the place suddenly became very quiet. She faced the two of them and addressed the President, looking straight into his eyes, "My name is Irene Wright, Mrs Irene Wright, and I am a widow. A little over a year ago, you hired my husband Ian, who was a computer expert and wrote programs that saved companies thousands of pounds. You poached him, and after he wrote programs that saved your company hundreds of thousands of pounds, you made him redundant. Do you remember him? No? Not even a flicker of recognition? He couldn't handle the rejection and killed himself. Familiar now? I made him a promise at his graveside that I would avenge him. He can rest in peace now. By the way, you can also call me 'Nemesis'."

There was an immediate stunned silence with wide eyes, gaping mouths and shaking of heads from both the President and the Sheikh. Irene then looked at the police and said, "You can take them away now."

Irene was at the police station, surrounded by Mike and his team. The Superintendent and the chief of police. Francois from Interpol was also there. They had booked their favourite pub for the night, and Interpol said they would foot the bill, food and drink until midnight. It was the most successful operation they had ever carried out, and the United Nations even sent congratulations and recognition for preventing a revolution in Venezuela. There was a lot to celebrate.

Halfway through the night, Francois looked at Irene, smiled at her and said, "You know what I'm going to say. Have you thought about it? My bosses are dead keen on you joining the organisation. You've got everything Interpol needs: a forensic accountant and an insolvency expert."

"Tell you what, Francois, it does appeal, but before I make my mind up, I need a holiday. I'll let you know when I return ok."

Liz was sitting right beside her, "Where do you want to go?"

"The last time I was in here, you and I had a great talk, and you told me about your adventures in the wilds of Canada; I fancy doing that."

"Well, if I had a plane, I'd fly you there myself."

"Shame about that; wait a minute, I know someone who owes me a big favour." She smiled and picked up her phone, got the connection and said, "Evening, Prime Minister, this is Irene Wright. Remember you asked if I ever needed anything?"

8.

A CHANGE IN DIRECTION

Irene was back and in Mike's office going over the events of the past few weeks. Relaxed and feeling refreshed after a well-deserved vacation, she wasn't the type of person to sit back and do nothing. She was also trying to decide where her future lay. Interpol was calling, but she wasn't sure.

The phone on Mike's desk rang, and he looked at it, then Irene, "Now that's unusual; that phone never rings; I use my mobile all the time."

"Suppose I'd better answer it; maybe I've won the Lottery."

Mike's eyebrows raised as he listened, then he looked at Irene and said, "It's for you."

"Is that you, Mrs Wright?"

"Yes - she didn't recognise the voice - who is this?"

"It's the Prime Minister; I knew you were back because you returned the plane you borrowed."

Irene got a little flustered.

"Thanks again, Mr Prime Minister."

"You're very welcome; after everything you did, you earned it. Reason for my call: I'd like to offer you a job. Can you make it to Downing Street tomorrow so we can discuss it?"

"Yes, sir, I can."

"Good; see you tomorrow at about eleven." And with that, he signed off.

"What was that all about?"

"That was the Prime Minister offering me a job; know what it's all about?"

"Not a clue; I haven't heard anything."

As Irene walked up to the front door at No. 10 Downing Street and went inside, a secretary was waiting for her. She smiled and said, "Good morning, Mrs Wright. The Prime Minister is waiting for you."

The office was larger than she thought, and there were two other people already there sitting at a table with two spare seats. File folders were placed in front of each seat.

A bit mystified, Irene turned to greet the Prime Minister. He shook her hand warmly and asked if she had a relaxing holiday and where she had gone. She told him that Liz, the drone pilot, had flown them to the wilds in Canada, where they hired a bush plane and flew to some of the hundreds of lakes in Northern Ontario, did some fishing and camped out. Said she'd love to return, smiled coyly and said, "Of course, I'd need a plane for that."

He smiled back. "We'll see, we'll see."

"Now, Mrs Wright, I'd like to introduce you to the Director General of the National Crime Agency, Sam Brown, and his Director of Investigations, Fred Turner."

We have recognised that you have unique skills, many of which we probably know nothing about. The way you were able to delve into information, sometimes hidden or wiped off a computer's memory, that somehow you were able to retrieve has impressed all of us.

You've uncovered a gun manufacturing business that uses the latest technology and an attempt to overthrow the Venezuelan Government that was very nearly successful. Plus, you've been able to place mostly illegal money from a Pyramid scheme into a hidden account amounting to close to a billion pounds. That money was being used to fund the revolution, and people in high places still can't find it and are waiting for you to divulge its location.

In short, Mrs Wright, we would like to offer you a position in the National Crime Agency."

Irene was taken aback. Not at all what she thought she was here for. She thought it might be an official thank you for what she had uncovered and replied, "That is very flattering and completely unexpected. I must tell you this is the second offer I've had since I returned. Interpol also asked me to join their organisation."

"I'm not surprised," the Prime Minister said.

Then the Director General spoke up, "Well, Mrs Wright that tells me because you haven't yet accepted, you are unsure about that vocation, and by the way, I must say, congratulations on an absolutely magnificent investigation. You've been able to accomplish something most people simply don't have the ability to do. We could certainly use your skills, Mrs Wright."

"Mr Brown, first of all, I'm not used to the formalities, and I'd feel more comfortable if you just called me Irene."

"I feel like you are one of the family already, Irene and thank you for that. I'm really intrigued at how you did what you did if I can put it that way. We have people in our cybercrimes unit who are specialists in that area, and I know they couldn't match your skills. Would you care to tell us how you did that?"

Irene smiled and said, "Now that would be telling, wouldn't it? Besides, you might not approve of my methods. I am rather unconventional, you know. The Prime Minister has probably told you that by profession, I am a Forensic Accountant, and I'm also an Insolvency Expert, which all helps."

"I won't pry any more, Irene, but I would like to offer you a position in the N.C.A. Heading up your own team in a new unit with the sole purpose of solving the unsolvable. Your immediate boss would be Fred Turner, Director of Investigations, sitting right beside me, and the next man above him would be myself. It's a new position, very demanding, very challenging and very rewarding. So, what do you say, Irene? Are you ready to commit yourself, need some more time, or is it not for you?"

"It's not how I imagined the day would turn out. I've been thinking about it as you spoke, and yes, it's for me, and I accept the position; thank you for offering it to me."

Everyone was delighted, handshakes all around, and the Prime Minister pulled out a bottle of bubbly from a fridge in the corner and toasted the new recruit to N.C.A.

There was idle chit chat, and then Fred Turner, Irene's new boss, suggested they all go out to dinner to celebrate and get to know each other better. The Prime Minister said, "Excellent idea, and we should eat here in Downing Street; we have an excellent chef. Is tonight too early for everyone? Good, we're all agreed. See you all tonight at 7.00 pm, and please let's make it informal."

Irene left Downing Street floating on air. She couldn't believe it and had to tell someone. She sent Mike and Liz a message: "Just left 10 Downing Street. I am now the Team Leader in a new unit set up to solve unsolvable crimes. I answer to the Director of Investigations, then the Director General of N.C.A. I pick my own team, and would you believe it? I'm having dinner tonight with the Prime

175

Minister, the Director General of N.C.A. and the Director of Investigations to celebrate and get to know each other."

It didn't take long to get a reply... *congrats from the team, the Chief and the Super, Mikey and Liz.*

It was Irene's first day at work, and her boss, Fred Turner was introducing her around. Everyone was told she was heading up a new unit to solve the unsolvable. Most people, when hearing that, just smiled and commented, good luck with that. Word quickly spread about who she was and what she had done, and that she was hand-picking her own team. That got a lot of interest.

After a two-week induction course, she was assigned an office and initially four desks on the floor outside. Her boss came around to see how she was settling in. Slowly, she said, slowly. Before I pick a team, I'd like to know what your most difficult case is, if it is active and if it is still outstanding. He smiled at her and said, "I'll be back in five minutes."

It actually took him a little longer, and he returned with several files under his arm. He put them on her desk and looked at her.

"This is one of the most violent and dangerous criminals we've ever been up against. His name is Larry Wilson, and he comes from Liverpool. We have never been able to catch up with him, arrest him or find his location. We know he operates out of different cities, but he's always one step ahead of us. It's almost as if he has a mole in the N.C.A.

He's a drug dealer and branching into cybercrime, although he's still not very good at it; despite all the experts we have, we still can't catch him. One other thing: cross him, and you're never heard of again."

"Sounds charming. Is there a picture of him?"

"Only one when he was a teenager, and that's not very clear. Any other picture is blurry or indistinct. He's a very careful man; doesn't let anyone take pictures of him."

"Better get on with it then, a lot of reading to do."

"You're sure you don't want any help?"

"Not yet, thanks; I have to feel my way first and get to know everything and everyone gradually. If I need 'anything' I'll let you know, ok."

With a smile, she looked at the folders, gave a big sigh, and picked up the first one.

The dossier in the file was full of his activities. Larry Wilson was certainly a thug of the first order, and from what she could see, violence was his middle name. From other criminals he did business with, she could see all transactions were in cash, with no exceptions. That meant he was either cash-rich or his money was tied up in stock. She doubted if he used banks. Perhaps he has bought the property and is operating out of that business or a chain of shops that would be a good way to launder money. She decided to take a different approach from everyone else. The N.C.A. liaised with other police forces, which gave her the idea of contacting Mike, but it was too early to ask his advice. Maybe when she had more information.

She decided to work backwards and looked for their last known location. It was a drug bust in Manchester. A small-time gang had bought a decent size quantity of drugs from Larry Wilson for local distribution. The problem for them was that the police had got wind of the deal long before it played out. Someone had a loose mouth. They walked right into a trap. The police described it as a very loose operation. It turned out everyone knew it was going down, and the police recovered £100K of cocaine as well as arresting ten criminals, two of them belonging to Larry Wilson's gang.

Now, she knew two of his gang, and she could get to work. All through the police interview, they kept Schtum. She wasn't surprised knowing of Wilson's reputation. It was her turn now. She started by looking at their histories. They appeared to be friends, although that's what she would expect. They were both serving a lengthy jail sentence, both in the same jail, and both married to sisters. One was called Alfie, and the other, being of Mexican ancestry, was called Pedro.

Irene knew their home addresses, and presuming they both had smart televisions, she had made a computer program with very advanced algorithms so that she could electronically look through any webcam they had in their houses and see what was going on. This was one of her little secrets that most people would flip out if they ever knew they could be observed in their own homes without the installation of spy cameras.

This wizardry paid off big time when she saw the two sisters sitting on a sofa talking to three men. They were talking about the arrival of a ship from South America with a very large shipment of cocaine for Larry Wilson. He had ordered double his usual quantity because of the increased demand. The sisters were going to make the payment in cash to the Colombian cartel, and the three men were the bodyguards. From the records, it was not mentioned that Alfie and Pedro's wives were heavily involved. No wonder the police were having difficulty shutting down their operation.

The ship was due to arrive in Liverpool a week Tuesday, and they were talking three tons of the stuff. They discussed the logistics of moving that quantity off the ship unnoticed. Turns out, the more she listened, the more she shook her head. Unbelievable, she kept on repeating, unbelievable. She had listened in at just the right time. They were revealing everything even that the ship had been specially built to hide drugs and other contraband. She had not used the office computer but her personal laptop that she had specially programmed and adapted.

No one could use it except herself, so if it was lost or stolen, her smartphone was connected, and she could easily locate it. These were all tools that she used as she worked for herself, and no one else was involved. Consequently, she didn't have to explain herself to anyone. That might have to change now that she worked for the N.C.A. She was a bit unsure what to tell them because her methods were highly controversial and probably frowned on apart from being a wee bit illegal. Take this latest information she had gathered. She had a copy because it was on her laptop, but did she show it or just pass on the details? She wasn't one hundred per cent sure it was legal.

One of the men got a phone call, and it was obvious it was the boss. Larry Wilson was arranging a meeting to go over the details of the pickup from the ship and how the women were going to make the payment to the Colombians. The man himself was going to hand over the cash, all in a camper van, to the women, who would then pay the Colombians. It was a one-sided conversation, but she was able to pick up enough of it to get most details.

This was one of those things that required immediate attention, but Irene had reservations. Fred Turner, when he was explaining how difficult it had been to arrest one of the biggest drug dealers in the country, half-jokingly said it was almost as if he had a spy in the N.C.A. In Irene's experience, that was a very real possibility. She had a thought and called her boss for a meeting right away.

Unfortunately, he was in a meeting with the Director General, and it was scheduled to last all day. Not good enough, she thought, her mind in turmoil, the best way forward. It didn't take her long to reach a decision. She smiled, not in humour but in resignation; this could be the shortest career ever.

She phoned the Director General, spoke to his secretary and told her to tell him it was urgent. She had to see both the D.G. and Fred Turner right away.

The D.G. frowned at the interruption, "I thought I said no interruptions, Sarah."

"Yes, Sir, but the new girl Irene insisted she had to see the two of you; it was very important."

"Well, with her track record, we'd best not ignore her; ask her to come in."

Irene knocked on the door and walked into the office.

"I apologise for the intrusion. I realise you are very busy, but I have come across time sensitive information about Larry Wilson that could lead to his arrest and prevent three tons of cocaine from coming into the country."

"Ok, let's hear it."

"There's only one thing I should explain first. I'm used to working on my own and doing things my way. I use a lot of computer programs and advanced algorithms that are of my own making, and my methods are unusual. Some of which you might not approve, and some might not be strictly legal. I'm not sure about that yet, so the method I used to get this information, I might keep to myself for the time being."

"I'm intrigued, Irene; I can't wait."

"Right, Larry Wilson has a ship specially built to smuggle drugs in secret compartments arriving from South America a week Tuesday and docking in Liverpool. It has three tons of cocaine hidden away on it. I don't know how much that is worth, but I think it is over five hundred million pounds sterling. He is paying for it in cash and using the wives of two of his men who were recently arrested and in jail to transfer the money in a VW camper van. The man himself is going to hand over the cash to the women, who in turn will pay the Colombians."

"One other thing, as I understand it, you've never been able to find Larry Wilson, let alone arrest him, and that is quite possibly because he was tipped off. You probably have a mole in your organisation. My suggestion is that for this operation, you keep the information to yourselves and use outside sources for the interception and arrests. The police unit I just left, headed by Inspector Mike O'Neil, would be ideal. I've been on operations with them before, and they are very efficient. You could use armed police, sworn to secrecy, for the interception of the camper van, and I would also suggest you bypass the police for the ship interception. In fact, tell no one about it and use 'Special Forces' for the interception. That way, the information is contained. You probably know the P.M. very well and can talk him into it. Imagine confiscating three tons of cocaine, five hundred million pounds in cash, arresting Larry Wilson, as well as impounding a ship designed specifically for smuggling drugs."

"Well, what do you think, have I still got a job?"

The Director General looked at Irene, a smile of satisfaction on his face.

"Well, young lady, you've definitely still got a job. You've been here five minutes, and we are on the verge of a very big breakthrough in the fight against organised crime. Well done. I would like it very much, as if it never took place, understand? It never took place if you showed me, one to one, how you use your special skills. I'm not going to say I will understand, but at least I would have an inkling of how you achieve what you do."

Irene looked at the D.G. for a long time, then said, "I'll think about it."

"Ok, Irene, we've got a lot of planning to do, and I agree that we try and keep it to ourselves, see if we can trap this Larry Wilson. I know you can trust the police Inspector you spoke about, but as you suggested, to keep as few people out of the loop as possible, can you speak to him face to face and make arrangements? I'll speak to the P.M. about intercepting the ship, and then we'll get together to go over the final plans. By the way, do you know the name of this ship?"

"Yes, it's called the S.S. Sterlitz."

She couldn't get through by phone, so she sent Mike a message that simply said, Urgent we meet a.s.a.p. and signed it, Irene. Her phone rang almost instantaneously, "How urgent?"

"Very urgent."

"How about now?"

"Be there in ten minutes."

She arrived rather breathless and, knowing the way, walked up to Mike's office, waving to people as she went. She sat down, and he said, "Well, what's got you in a flap?"

"Nice to see you too."

"Sorry, didn't mean to be so abrupt. What's going on?"

"First of all, this is top secret. I don't mean to be dramatic, but we worry there might be a leak in the N.C.A., and I convinced the D.G. that we should involve you. In fact, maybe we should get the Superintendent in here as well."

"It's that big?"

"Yes, Mike."

"Right, I'll go and get him. He's just down the hall."

The Superintendent and Mike walked briskly into the office, and handshakes were exchanged.

"Sorry for the dramatics, but we have to move fast. Have you heard of Larry Wilson?"

"That slippery weasel, who hasn't."

"Well, this is what we've discovered."

Irene then related how she had used her computer programs and special algorithms to find out about the drug shipment and Larry Wilson handing over £500 million in cash in a camper van to the wives of two of his men currently incarcerated in a high-security prison. "He is doing this in person, and the wives, in turn, are going to pay the Colombians. It's a specially designed ship built to hide drugs. This shipment of cocaine is landing in Liverpool in a week, and the D.G. has asked the Prime Minister to get Special Forces to intercept the ship. We are trying to keep the number of people involved to a minimum because of the possibility of a mole in the organisation."

"What we would like is a police armed response unit to intervene when the cash is given to the two women. Who it is can be withheld from armed response until the last minute, but it will be your team, so you can control it."

"My, my, you haven't stopped, have you? Well done, Irene. Mike and I can sort out the details. It will give us all great pleasure to finally get Larry Wilson behind bars. Mike can liaise as we go along."

It was the day before the S.S. Sterlitz was due to dock. Irene had found out the arrival time, and Special Forces had picked their spots waiting for the ship. They had spotted a lookout staked out at the end of the dock and kept a close eye on him. They would lift him before they descended on the ship so he couldn't give a warning.

Mike had his Armed Response team organised and ready to go; all he needed was the time and place of the handover.

Irene was using her technology to monitor the sisters and was rewarded with the information she needed. Larry Wilson was meeting them at a busy shopping centre at noon, the busiest time of the day at the entrance to the mall. He was crafty and hadn't stayed free for no reason at all. This was the busiest time of day, and the location was practically gridlocked with people rushing about.

Mike had the same thoughts as everyone else. Larry Wilson would meet the sisters, hand over the keys and melt into the crowd. He would have minders all around to protect the money. Irene said there would be three and had provided pictures of the sisters and the three minders. How she had done that, he didn't know, and he doubted she would tell him. They now had the advantage of knowing what they looked like. He put tails on the sisters as soon as they left for the mall.

Everyone was in communication with each other. The SS Sterlitz had docked, and Special Forces were waiting for word from Mike before they boarded. The sisters were on their way to the mall, closely followed by three of Mike's team. A V.W. Camper van was spotted entering the Mall and instantly shadowed. It parked in a busy spot, and the two sisters approached the driver. He got out and started talking to them. The conversation lasted about one minute, at which time he was surrounded by armed police who had left cover of vans and cars. Mike called Special Forces and gave them the go-ahead. The first thing they did was lift the lookout, who got the fright of his life, and then they boarded the ship.

Larry Wilson was startled. Not expecting any trouble, he had planned it perfectly. With the pictures Irene had provided, his three men had been fingered early on and quickly arrested as their boss was apprehended. The sisters were flummoxed and readily put their hands in the air. All danger of a shootout over, the mall was flooded by regular police who took charge of the camper van.

A relieved Mike phoned Irene, who was waiting anxiously in the D.G.'s office with Fred Turner.

"Good news, no problems, we've arrested Larry Wilson, and the camper van is full of bundles of cash. Special Forces have just boarded the S.S. Sterlitz, and when I get an update, I'll call you back." Another loud cheer came from the D.G.'s office, and everyone knew something was going on but didn't know what.

Special Forces were making their way slowly through the SS Sterlitz. They had encountered a little resistance but nothing major. No one thought they would be boarded and searched. Knowing there were secret compartments, it didn't take too long to find the first batch of cocaine. Smiles of satisfaction all around, and a few hours later, they were looking at three tons of pure Colombian cocaine. The major in charge phoned Mike with the news and asked for transport to remove and store it in a high-security facility.

Mike phoned Irene and told her they had found the cocaine. Another loud cheer came from D.G.'s office. The news quickly spread through the N.C.A. offices, and everyone was looking at the new employee quite differently and knowing she was hiring her own team; all wanted to be part of it. The D.G. even got a phone call of congratulations from the Prime Minister as he had sanctioned the use of Special Forces and had been keeping an eye on how things were progressing.

Mike smiled very broadly. She has done it again, and this definitely calls for another celebration. This time, he was beaten to the punch by the N.C.A. Fred Turner phoned and suggested a get-together of the two teams with them footing the bill. They were all in high spirits. "What a result," is all everyone could say.

Their local pub was booked for the night and quickly filled up with both law enforcement agencies. Irene was not a gregarious person and preferred to be quiet and low-key, but she was the centre of attention. She was having trouble fielding all the questions about how she was able to provide the information for the operation against Larry Wilson. In the end, she just told everyone she had an informant.

Irene was in a corner talking to Liz and two members of her team when she noticed someone edging their way through the crowd clutching a large brown folder. His eyes were darting everywhere, obviously looking for someone. He was stocky and well-dressed, then his eyes lit on Irene, and he headed straight for her.

"Are you Irene?"

"Yes, can I help you?"

"I've been told to give you this package."

"Who are you, and who told you to give me this package? What's in it? What is this all about?"

By this time, Mike and Fred, who had been talking not far away, noticed the intrusion, and neither knew who it was, so they went over to join the group. The stranger was talking to Irene by then.

"My name is Alfonso. I work for Interpol. My boss tried to recruit you, and he said you would be the best person to know what to do."

"OK, but first of all, I want to see some identification, and I want your boss' phone number."

"Of course, forgive me. I should have introduced myself first."

He produced his credentials, which were examined by Irene, Mike, and Fred and pronounced kosher. Irene then took his boss's phone number and called him on an open Mike so that everyone could hear. The phone rang, and Irene said, "Irene Wright here; you sent Alfonso with a package; what's that all about?"

"I apologise for the roundabout way of doing this, but I heard you were celebrating a big win, and I thought this might be the quickest way to reach you."

"What is wrong with going through normal channels? You know I am no longer freelance but work for the N.C.A. This is rather unorthodox and, I must say annoying; we are in a pub celebrating and to be interrupted in this way is just not acceptable."

"Again, I apologise. This is an intercept from the secret world of spies. It flashed up red in more than one inbox, and no one here, with all our experts, can make head nor tail of it, but we know it is important because it has been given a code name Barbarossa and is increasingly mentioned in top secret communiques. It is important because it concerns strategies by the Russians in the

Ukraine war and seems to target the U.K. if you look at it yourself."

"Well, my friend, my boss just happens to be standing right beside me and I don't think this fits in my job description. I now work for the N.C.A., not the G.C.H.Q. or Interpol. Tell you what I'll do. I'll give it a quick once over, with my boss's permission and let you know if it's worth pursuing, OK?"

"I understand; please look kindly on me, Irene."

"Ok, I'll be in touch one way or the other. Goodnight."

They all looked at each other, no one saying a word; then Irene said, "I'm enjoying myself; I don't really want to interrupt this get together to look at whatever is in this folder," Liz said, "Could be important."

"Trouble is if I look at what's in there, I'd then be obliged to follow it through. It beats me why, with all the experts they have someone can't decipher what it is all about or are they too lazy. What's it to be Fred, you're my boss?"

"Tough call Irene, we are National Crime. This sounds more like international conspiracies."

Mike then interrupted, "Sounds like Interpol is sufficiently worried at what's been intercepted. They can't solve it and feel Irene can. If it's about Russia, Ukraine and the U.K., we are bound to be affected. I would say it is a favour from one agency to another. There's always a payback time. The bottom line seems important enough for the powers to be to interrupt our celebrations. I'd say look at it. Trouble is it's all falling on one person, Irene. She's the one to decide, probably not if but when."

All eyes were on Irene, who shook her head slowly from side to side and said, "Shit, it's all down to me then, isn't it!"

Irene put down her drink opened the folder, and started reading. She changed, sheer concentration now. It took her about one minute to briefly scan the contents, then she put everything back in the folder, looked up and said, "I was afraid of this. I'm going to need a computer, Shit! Shit! Shit! 'I can't put if off. My laptop is in my apartment; I'll need it'."

"I've got my laptop in my car outside. You can use that."

"Thanks, Mike, but I need my laptop; it has special programs. I need them, and only I can use them."

"I can get someone to pick it up."

"Irene frowned, not a good idea, I'll have to go myself, damn."

"Can it wait until tomorrow?"

"If I hadn't read it, I'd say yes, but right now, the answer is no. Can someone drive me to my apartment?"

"No problem, I'll get a police driver to take you right away."

Then, Fred said, "What's so important you have to drop everything and attend to it?"

"I know you are my boss and all, and I mean no offence by this, but I can't say anything about it until I get clearance from much higher up and by much higher up, I mean the Foreign Secretary or the Prime Minister."

"Wow, what a way to spoil a party. Any help you need, Irene, just say the word."

"The same goes for us, just ask."

Mike said, "I'll organise a police driver right now. Are you going to stay at your place? You could work from the station, whatever you want."

"I think it best to work from the N.C.A. But thanks. This is a completely new ball game. It involves different rules, foreign governments, and not friendly ones at that. It's about deciphering and protecting the information that's in this folder. Sorry I'm being so mysterious, but I can understand what it is about, and it is serious."

After Irene had left with the police driver, they all looked at each other, and then Fred said, "Who is this girl?"

Mike smiled and said, "We call her Lara Croft."

It was ten thirty p.m. when Irene left the apartment with her laptop. She was now completely sober and fully alert, her mind whirring at what was ahead of her and the best approach. She signed into the N.C.A. office and asked the security staff to be particularly alert and patrol the building on a frequent and intermittent basis; then, she headed for her office.

In the meantime, Fred decided that if Interpol was on alert and Irene decided it was serious enough to go into work, regardless of the time, he should phone the Director General. The party was in full swing in the pub, but everyone was talking about the latest developments and what it was all about. Alfonso, in the meantime, had disappeared, so no one could question him, and it was all guesswork, but everyone knew from past experience that both the police and the N.C.A., not to mention Interpol were going to get busy.

Irene was in the dark web doing things with her programs that were able to interpret what was uninterpretable to everyone else. She heard the door leading to her office open and guessed it was security doing their patrols, but she sensed the presence of someone approaching her office and looked up. The Director General was walking towards her. She closed everything down on her laptop. What she did was for her eyes only.

"I understand there's a bit of a flap on Irene," he said,

"The signals that are being sent have been heavily disguised making it extremely difficult to interpret. No wonder Interpol was worried. Luckily, I have programs that can solve most signals designed to confuse anyone trying to read them, and I can write algorithms for the others. That's what I'm doing right now. I don't want to say too much until I get the gist of what's going on. I can tell you it is pretty serious and I should know much more in the next few hours."

"Can you give me a hint?"

"What I can say is that we will have to get the Prime Minister active on this because it involves National Security. Russia and Iran are conspiring against Ukraine. There is nothing new there, but the U.K. is somehow involved, and that's what I have to work out as well as what's going on. When I know that, I'll let you know. I'll be working straight through until I get some answers, Ok?"

"You are certainly dedicated, Irene; don't overdo it. I'll see you shortly."

Irene fired up her laptop after the D.G. left. She was on the dark web and had just intercepted another message that was encrypted, but the source was London this time, not entering the country. The encryption was also slightly different, pointing out a new user. She was fully alert now. Something had changed.

Her heart started racing as she deciphered the message. My God, she thought, the P.M. is going to flip out. This new user was giving her information that made sense of the previous messages she had deciphered, and Interpol couldn't make head nor tail of.

This calls for a red alert or whatever the government calls it. She started writing out a report rather than verbalise it. My God, she thought again, what is the world coming to? She addressed it to the P.M.

Dear Prime Minister,

I have to make you aware of an imminent threat to the U.K. Various messages have been intercepted by Interpol that made them sufficiently worried to ask for help as they had trouble deciphering the content. The operation was given the code name "Barbarossa". I don't know if they gave it that title or that is the name given by the perpetrators.

This is what I have deciphered and understand from the messages. Russia and Iran have conspired to use Iranian made "Shahed - 136 Drones" in an attack on the U.K. They are going to smuggle ten drones into the country, store them in a disused R.A.F. Base in Machrihanish on the tip of the Mull of Kintyre, now used as a local airport and use eight of them to attack the House of Commons and the other two to attack the Ukrainian Embassy in London.

The drones will be shipped on a boat with its final destination Russia. It contains parts and equipment to help Russia build their own drone factory. The ship will meet a small freighter at a predetermined longitude/latitude in the Atlantic and transfer the drones, which will take them to a port in the UK. I don't have the name of the port yet. They will then be taken by road to Machrihanish. I presume the ship is Russian. I'll get that information later on.

The drones themselves are propeller driven, 3.5m long, 2.5 wide, and weigh 200 kg. Their range is approx. 1200 miles, they fly at a speed of 185 km/hour and have a ceiling of 4,000 m. The payload is anything from 36 to 80 kg of high explosives. The distance from Machrihanish to London is 550 miles. For a guidance system, they use a computer processor built by a U.S. company. Therefore, they are able to somehow overcome sanctions and receive vital components for their drones. That's something that should be looked into. The drones will be programmed in Machrihanish so I presume it will be someone from the Islamic Students Association who will do that.

The latest message came from the Islamic Student Association located in London. The Iranian Republic has been using this student Association to foment unrest among other students. I assume the Home Office/Foreign Office are both aware of this.

I can pass on other details but crucially I don't know the timing. From other messages it could be after the summer recess in early September when the House will have a maximum number of members present. This is mentioned as a favourite timing.

That is all I have just now but will continue to monitor the sites and report as information becomes available.

May I make an early judgement and suggestion? Once the drones have been transferred to the freighter, Ukraine can attack the ship as a legitimate target using their new found and homemade marine drones they have used successfully in the Black Sea against a Russian warship and freighter. That ship by the way is not only transporting the ten drones destined for the U.K. but also hundreds of Iranian drones to be used against Ukraine. All the more reason for Ukraine to prevent further destruction in their country.

Sincerely Irene Wright

She printed the report, put it in an envelope and addressed it to the D.G. she wrote on the outside after you read this, can you make sure the P.M. gets it? I'm off to bed; I'll be in later. Signed it Irene and… it is now five a.m.

The D.G. came into the office at six a.m., read the letter, said, "Holy shit!" and phoned Fred to get in as fast as he could.

9.

THE CONSPIRACY

Irene had a good sleep and was ready to go into the office at noon. As she left her apartment building, she noticed a police car waiting outside and as soon as she appeared, the passenger door opened and a police officer came out. She could see he was one of the armed response team and wondered what had happened. As she walked down the brief set of stairs, he opened the rear door, smiled and said, "I presume you are Mrs Wright?"

Irene acknowledged, and the police officer told her he had been assigned to escort her to Downing Street as soon as she appeared.

She had not expected this and thought it was a bit over the top; however, as the car approached Downing Street, she saw the street was a beehive of activity, and for the first time, she saw an armed vehicle outside No.10. The police officer walked side by side right into the building and passed her off to a security guard who didn't smile just said the Prime Minister is waiting for you, please follow me.

She was a bit mystified at the precautions being taken and the serious looks on people's faces as they almost scurried about clutching papers. The security guard knocked on the door marked P. M's Office and waited. After a minute, it slowly opened. A face looked out, took in the security guard and Irene and motioned them inside.

As Irene walked in, at a glance, she didn't think anyone else could fit in the room. All conversation stopped as she appeared, and then the Prime Minister stood up from the head of the table and walked towards her hand outstretched with a warm smile on his face.

"Well done, Irene, well done. Come and sit beside me. Everyone, this is Irene Wright, the author of this report and an absolute wizard at interpretation. She was able to take the hieroglyphics sent by the opposition to confuse us and make it, in their eyes impossible to understand to a coherent analysis of what we are facing. Irene, you probably recognise some of the faces here. Are you ok with taking some questions?"

"To a point, although there are some questions if asked, I won't be able to answer, OK?"

The Prime Minister smiled and understood. She had to keep her methods to herself, "Of course, it is Irene; I understand completely."

Irene looked around and was relieved to see Mike and her boss, Ted, as well as the Chief of Police.

The man next to the P.M. introduced himself, "Irene, I'm George Walker, the Home Secretary; first of all, congratulations on accomplishing what seemed an impossible job. I know how hard it was because I've had teams of experts trying to crack these codes. I, and I'm sure everyone else, would like to know how you did it and if we can rely on your interpretation."

There was a sudden silence. No one was expecting a challenge of this nature. The Prime Minister spoke up.

"George, I'm astonished at your attitude. Irene, you don't have to answer that."

"No, Prime Minister, I'd like to reply."

She looked directly at the Home Secretary. Mike recognised the subtle change in Irene's features and felt sorry for George Walker.

"Mr Walker, first of all, I'd like you to show me the same courtesy I showed you during your petulant little diatribe by just listening and absorbing what I have to say."

There was a noticeable sharp intake of breath from more than one of those present. Irene carried on, "By vocation, I am a forensic accountant and an insolvency expert. I develop my own computer programs and use algorithms to analyse and interpret communications that need interpretation. I used all of these tools in my work, and they formed the basis of my report to the Prime Minister. You are now questioning the validity of that report. It is not my fault that your so-called experts don't know what they are doing. By simply applying common sense to creating an algorithm, your 'Experts' should have been able to interpret the communications. It is blatantly obvious that they are clueless; in fact, do they even understand what an algorithm is and what they do? I have my doubts that even you understand what they are even though you hired the so-called experts.

I will gladly explain my conclusions, but not to people like you who use their lack of knowledge to bluff, bluster and try to prove their superiority on a subject they know nothing about and try to repudiate a valid conclusion.

Mr Walker, this is a real threat to the U.K. from Russia and the Islamic Revolutionary Guard who, as you should be aware as Home Secretary, spread anti-Semitic propaganda in the U.K. universities via the Islamic Students Association in London. The same association that sent several speakers to address student audiences across Britain, trying to radicalise them. Some of these speakers claim the holocaust was fake and advocate violence against Jews in an apocalyptic war. There are recordings of these speeches, and Britain has sanctioned the speakers for Human Rights Abuses. I certainly hope you are aware of this.

These are the people who will be arming and programming the drones that will strike the House and the

Ukrainian Embassy. I suggest you pay my report a little more attention rather than immediately dismiss it."

There was complete silence. No one knew how to proceed, then Mike spoke up, "My name is Inspector Mike O'Neil, and I support Irene 100%. In my short association with her, she discovered a gun manufacturing centre based on the latest 3D technology that we were able to put an end to and an illegal pyramid scheme where the criminal fraternity had invested hundreds of millions of pounds. She closed that down and transferred the money into a special account that no one could find. She said it is hiding in open sight and will stay there until we are able to trace the so-called investors. I would never question her capabilities, and as a police force, we are actively investigating her latest findings."

The Prime Minister finally spoke, "I would also like to add my support and say we are fortunate to have someone with her capabilities on our side."

At that, George Walker stood up and apologised for any offence, excused himself and left the room.

The next day, he tendered his resignation as Home Secretary. The general opinion was that it was not voluntary.

Miles away in the Port of Bandar Abbas, which was the main maritime port of Iran, there was frenzied activity centred around one ship, the MV Sparta 1V. It was a

Russian-built cargo ship capable of carrying a maximum load of 8,600 tons. Military experts had long suspected it of carrying weapons for the war in Ukraine. The last container put in place was the one to be offloaded at sea and held ten Iranian-built Shahed - 136 Drones.

The ship's final destination was St Petersburg, Russia. The bulk of the shipment was Iranian-built drones to be used by Russia for their war against Ukraine. The rest were modules to build a factory so that Russia could make their own drones. There was a time schedule, so the ship had to leave at a specific time and date. Everything was worked out, from leaving Bandar Abbas to the final accomplishment. It was 8,500 nautical miles to St. Petersburg, and that meant 35 days at sea through the Suez, the Med., and into the Atlantic. The transfer would be made somewhere in the Atlantic. The exact timing still had to be finalised, so the ship needed to leave Iran on time.

Irene was now back in her office, working her way through the flurry of messages going to and from the Islamic Students Association. There was once again a different operator, and it would appear this new arrival was the one in charge. He was making sure the special container was on board the M.V. Sparta 1V. The reply had just come in, "Loaded and tied down, ship sails on the morning tide." This time, she got his call sign. He was known as "Desert Hawk". That's going to make it easier, she thought. There was a meeting at Downing Street in thirty minutes for an update. She gathered everything she had and headed out the door. She had been assigned an armed guard, and he and his partner were waiting outside to take her wherever she wanted. Trevor opened the rear door and raised his eyebrow in a question. She said Downing Street, and they drove off.

Irene was taken to the P.M.'s office immediately, and the chosen few were sitting around a table looking anxious. There was no preamble. She started in right away, "The latest I know is the ship bringing the drones is a Russian registered cargo ship with an apparent dubious history of transporting weapons. It is the M.V. Sparta 1V, and it has just finished loading its last container. That's the one to be transferred mid-Atlantic to a small freighter, destination Mull of Kintyre. It is currently in Iran and sailing on the morning tide. I think the person in charge is in London right now and goes by the name of 'Desert Hawk'."

"It will take the ship approximately 35 days to reach St Petersburg, so it should be mid-Atlantic in about three weeks. Our problem is tracing its movements. A treaty known as the International Convention for the Safety of Life at Sea requires large ships to have automatic identification systems (A.I.S.). This gives other ships and coastal authorities the vessel's name, heading, speed and other information. It should not be turned off. It is a tool used to evade sanctions and can be used for ship-to-ship transfers at sea where the ship's position cannot be seen.

That leaves us with the problem of knowing where it is when they turn it off. Transporting drones to be used against Ukraine makes that ship a legitimate target, according to Ukraine. So, it is within the realm of possibility that they are going to attack the M.V. Sparta 1V. If they do, I wouldn't blame them. I even support the idea."

The Prime Minister looked around the room then at Irene and said, "That's something we have to discuss with our Ukrainian friends, although I doubt they will confirm or deny their intentions."

"I would like to add that my boss, Fred Turner, is away investigating the holiday complex and other sites on the Mull of Kintyre for possible storage and launching positions. What we have to keep in mind is that while the airfield at Machrihanish is ideal for launching drones, the 'Shahed – 136' can be launched from an almost vertical position, and they usually are from battlefield conditions, but you need a gantry for that and they usually launch five at a time. Whether this container includes gantries or not, I do not know."

The Prime Minister shook his head from side to side, "How you are able to get hold of this information and put it all together is beyond me. You're doing a great job. Keep in touch with anything new. You have my private phone number if anything major changes."

"Thank you, I will. Now I'd better be off and see if there are any new messages."

As she left Downing Street, her phone rang, a quick glance and she could see it was Mike, when she said Hi, he replied, "It's lunchtime, and before you burn yourself out how about joining myself and a few members of the team for a bite to eat at our local?"

"Right now, nothing would give me greater pleasure. I'm on the road and will be there in ten minutes."

As the protection car pulled up outside the pub, the team were just entering. Almost as one, they turned around as Trevor was opening the door for Irene. They conversed briefly, and she joined the group. Smiles and hugs all around, and as the car drove off, Trevor was left behind.

They placed their order and over drinks, everyone wanted to know how she was enjoying working at the N.C.A. then one of them said what's with the protection car? Liz added isn't that the man who helped you out of the car? Pointing out the man sitting by himself eating a sandwich.

"Oh, that's Trevor, my protection officer."

There were a few giggles, and someone suggested it was the other way around.

Irene smiled and said, "No, it's the case we're working on just now. It's pretty heavy, and Trevor has been assigned to me until it is over."

"Suppose you can't tell us what it's all about?" Irene just smiled.

They parted company after lunch, with Irene hugging them all and thanking them all for the get-together and a promise to do it again once the case was over. Mike hung around after everyone had left.

"Anything new?"

She kept him up to date and said it was starting to unfold pretty rapidly. The Islamic Students Association appeared to be the centre of activities, and someone with the call sign "Desert Hawk" looked to be the man in charge.

"Why weren't you at the last meeting?"

"Don't really know why. Maybe you have to be higher up the chain to get a regular invite."

"That is ridiculous. You and your team are going to be doing most of the investigating, and you should already be heavily immersed in that. I'll find out what's happening and be prepared; that ship is going to be mid-Atlantic in a couple of weeks."

When she arrived back at the office, she first of all asked her boss, Fred Turner, if he knew why Mike had not been invited to the last meeting. He said he was surprised himself but thought he had something prearranged going on. That made her think, and she went over all the participants from the previous meetings and Mike was the only one left out.

Now she was curious, and she phoned the P.M.'s secretary to find out who made out the invite lists for meetings about "Operation Barbarossa". She came back almost immediately. "It was the Secretary of Defence."

"Do you have any idea why Inspector Mike O'Neill was left off the list?"

"Because of the nature of the problem, the P.M. thought the likeliest person to control the events was Joe Banks, the Secretary of Defence."

"That doesn't really answer the question. Do you have any idea why the Inspector was left off the list?"

There was a pause, and Irene heard the slight hesitation in the secretary's voice and interrupted, "You have no idea how important this is. I need an honest answer and don't worry, this is just between the two of us."

"The rumour is that Joe Banks does not like Inspector O'Neill because of some operation he headed involving gun manufacturing that affected national security, according to Joe Banks and Inspector O'Neill took the recognition."

"Thank you, that is really helpful." That was about the 3D gun manufacturing Irene had discovered, but said nothing to the secretary. She then decided it was time to investigate Joe Banks. The Dark Web made it much simpler and she quickly raced through his qualifications and achievements. Everything seemed normal and above board until she spotted one entry. Her pulse quickly escalated. On his first major political appointment, he was asked to list his favourite books, and he included an obscure listing of rising stars and their achievements. This listing stood out like a sore thumb and drew her right to it. Most people listed the classics, books that they had never even looked at, never mind read, but it looked good on their resume.

It was a magazine, and she had the devil's own job tracing a copy. Finally, she found one in the British Library. It listed rising stars in the business and political world and their claim to fame. Included in that magazine was one Joe Banks, a rising politician. The more Irene read, the faster her breathing became. The vanity of the man was about to be his downfall.

She couldn't believe what the magazine was revealing. Joe Banks had worked in Saudi Arabia for five years and was a fluent Arabic speaker. At the time of normalising ties between Iran and Saudi Arabia, he had worked in Tehran to help in the negotiations.

Iran's supreme leader, Ayatollah Ali Khamenei, was dedicated to achieving the Regime's grand ambition to restore an Islamic Civilisation. The U.S. and the liberal International Order have always been seen by him as the ultimate obstacle - The Great Satan. The Ayatollah viewed the normalisation of ties to be far more about facilitating, along with China and Russia, the rise of a new anti-Western Global Order. Joe Banks' claim to fame then, knowingly or not, was helping him to achieve that ambition. He was noted in the magazine as a rising political star with influence who had worked in Tehran to help normalise ties with Saudi Arabia.

Irene checked the Register in the House of Commons, and there was no mention of him being an Arabic speaker or his role in normalising ties between Iran and Saudi Arabia. My God, she thought, by a sheer fluke, he was now exposed. The Prime Minister is really going to flip out this time. She printed out copies of what she had found, put together a quick resume and practically ran into Fred's office.

He looked at her with alarm as she blurted out, "We have to see the D.G. right away, then it is full speed to Downing Street."

She then went through her findings, and Fred phoned the D.G. immediately and asked him to get into his office as quickly as he could. As they waited, he said, "This has massive implications."

She suggested Mike accompany them to the P.M. He agreed, and Irene quickly phoned him. He answered, "Yes, Irene, is it urgent?"

"More than you could ever guess. Can you get to my office as quickly as possible?"

"Blues and Twos?"

"Absolutely!"

The D.G. was flabbergasted and agreed they had to see the P.M. immediately. He phoned his private number. It was answered on the first ring. The D.G. said, "This is really urgent. We have to meet right away."

"I have an important meeting with some ambassadors in five minutes. Sam, can it wait?"

"Absolutely not. You won't believe what I have to tell you. Irene has discovered something that will shake you to the core."

"Can you tell me what it's about?"

"Best not, face to face only."

"Ok, see you shortly."

With perfect timing, Mike rushed into the office. They left together, with Irene explaining I'll fill you in as we go.

The Prime Minister was pacing up and down his office as they arrived. "So, tell me."

The D.G. said, "Probably best to let Irene explain."

"It was a sheer fluke that I discovered this. I wondered why Mike was not at the last meeting and, on closer inspection, found he was the only one excluded. The Secretary of Defence had omitted him from the list in a fit of pique. He felt he should have been mentioned in the 3D gun manufacturing business we broke up even though he had nothing to do with it, so I investigated possible reasons and discovered he is a fluent Arabic speaker, worked in

Saudi Arabia for five years, then worked for Iran to formalise ties between Iran and Saudi. This is not mentioned anywhere in the Commons Register. I have printouts of the details. Now we have the situation of Iranian drones targeting the House of Commons and the Ukrainian Embassy."

"Let me read your material, Irene and everyone. Please sit down while I go through it." He had an afterthought and buzzed his secretary to come in.

"Can you find out where Joe Banks is right now without making him aware you asked? Thanks."

The P.M. spent the next five minutes going over the printouts, absorbing everything, then vehemently saying just one word, "Shit!" The expletive summed it up and needed no more explanation.

"Irene, I don't know how you do it. We have to act fast, given the current situation." At that point, his secretary came in and said he was in his office in the Commons.

The Prime Minister then turned to Mike, "I'm going to have Joe Banks arrested; perhaps you could liaise with Serious Crimes, alright? You and your people are about to get very busy.

In the absence of a Home Office Minister at present, Mike, can you take charge of investigating the Islamic Student Association and try to find who this 'Desert Hawk' is? I don't need to tell you what to do. You know better than me. Everything is at your disposal. Whatever you need, just ask. I'm going to give you written authority. Anyone gives you hassle, tell them to phone me directly. I'll phone your chief as soon as you leave, telling him what's happening.

Sam, Fred, you also know better than me what to do, and of course, whatever you need, just ask. I'll give you instructions confirming that."

"Irene, what can I say? Perhaps you could make yourself available to everyone if they need you. Thank you all very much."

Mike then said, "We should get together and plan a course of action; I suggest we leave here and meet at the station. Does everyone agree?"

Fred said, "Yes, initially, I can see the sense of that, but we might have more resources at hand. I suppose we'll just play it by ear. Let's go to your station to start with."

The P.M. had phoned the chief, so he was aware of what was going on when everyone came in. Mike commandeered the meeting room and called his team in. He explained the situation, and they were to drop everything they were doing and concentrate on finding out what they could about the Islamic Students Association. He cautioned them that they were very dangerous and on a mission to destroy the West. Their immediate goal was to send drones into the House of Commons and the

Ukrainian Embassy. Irene's protection officer, Trevor, was always close, saying nothing, eyes darting everywhere. His presence brought a sober reality of what was happening home to the detectives.

Irene found a space and started looking for messages on her laptop. "Desert Hawk" was sending instructions. He wanted the storage facilities at Machrihanish finalised and fully operational within the week. She passed this on to Fred and Mike. Fred was just there and said all the wigwam units had been reserved, and two of the large cabins. Irene had a thought and singled out Liz, "Can you fly helicopters, particularly attack helicopters?"

"Yes, what are you thinking?"

"Just planning for every eventuality."

Irene was back at her laptop looking for messages when there was a sudden flurry of activity on the dark web. She recognised the signature; it was Desert Hawk, but it was going to take her a few minutes to decipher. There was one message in particular that he had sent that was very important, so she concentrated on that. It was an instruction to the captain of the M.V. Sparta 1V. The ship was just leaving the Suez Canal and entering the Mediterranean, and he had been told to turn off the A.I.S. and leave it off until further notice. It was highly dangerous because the Mediterranean was very busy with shipping, and the traffic relied on the recognition system as a safety device.

She rushed into the meeting room, "The ship is in the Med heading for the Atlantic with its A.I.S. turned off. Liz, can you get a drone, preferably one that's armed, and follow it before we lose it? I'll clear it with the P.M."

"Right, on my way, be in touch when I'm in the air."

Irene went back to her office and started working on her laptop again. Fred and the D.G. looked at each other and then at Mike, a look of almost bewilderment on their faces. Everyone else seemed oblivious to what was happening and were working away. Even the police chief had his sleeves rolled up and busy on the phone. Mike smiled at them and said, "I told you, she's Lara Croft."

10.

DESERT HAWK

More messages were being sent to "Desert Hawk". The Ukrainian Embassy was being cased from the outside, presumably by so-called students from the Islamic Students Association. "They made a mistake by saying that we had changed into Western clothes, and Sheila was wearing a jacket that said - Down with Putin - to easily blend in with people mingling outside the Ukrainian embassy."

"Got them!" Irene rushed into the Meeting Room again.

"Mike, they've just made a big mistake, messages going to Desert Hawk identify two people, a male, and a female, wearing a jacket that says, 'Down with Putin'. They thought that would make them blend in. They're outside the Ukrainian embassy right now."

Mike said, "Magic, I'm on the way, want to come?"

He directed the last comment at Fred, who jumped to his feet and said, "You bet!"

They ran out with another two of his team who were also in the room.

The D.G. looked at Irene, smiled and said, "You're a regular ball of fire."

Irene returned the smile and said, "Got to get back; they're starting to make mistakes."

Mike arrived at the Ukrainian Embassy in an unmarked police car, let off his two detectives at one end of the street, and drove to the other end. The road was fairly busy, with several people milling about in front of the building. Fred saw the girl right away and nudged Mike, nodding his head in her direction. Mike radioed his detectives and said, "We have to make sure we get the man as well. The four of them converged from different directions, and then one of his detectives saw a man sidle up to the woman, 'Got Him'," he radioed.

Mike told them, "We do this together; be careful. They might be armed, more than likely knives and make sure they don't do a runner; right, let's go." They were alert but not expecting a confrontation. Mike and Fred grabbed the man by the arms, wrestled him to the ground, and got the cuffs on him. At the same time, the two detectives grabbed the woman, but she started screaming and kicking out and sank her teeth into one of the detective's hands. He grimaced but held on, and they managed to get her to the ground and handcuff her. Mike called for the paddy wagon, which the chief had anticipated they might need, and had it waiting just around the corner.

Mike looked at the detective's hand, "She's broken the skin. You have to go to the hospital right away and get a tetanus shot and whatever other attention you might need. I'll call for a car. In fact, I don't need to do that. There's one now."

He called the chief and told him they got the two of them, and they were on their way to the station. It might be an idea to give their phones to Irene. She's quite technically advanced and see if she can get anything out of them while they are fresh. "Harry, one of my detectives, got bitten on the hand by the woman and is on his way to the hospital for treatment; otherwise, we are all okay. See you shortly."

Fred got out his phone and said to Mike, "I think we might need the serious crime squad. No telling what Irene has uncovered since we've been gone, do you agree?"

"Yes, do it. I just hope no one has told the press about the arrests, that would screw things up. We don't want to alert 'Desert Hawk' until we know more about those drones."

When Mike and Fred got back to the station a truck from the M.O.D. was making a delivery. Several boxes were piled on top of a large dolly, and the chief was outside talking to the driver and another man. Both wore white overalls that Mike thought was quite unusual. As they approached, the chief said, "Ah, Mike, you came back at the right time. Turns out that Liz is now the pilot of an MQ-9 Reaper. These gentlemen have been sent to set up a video link so we can see what it is looking at. Irene will explain all about it."

Fred said, "Isn't Liz one of your detectives? She was in the meeting room."

"Yes, she is; she is also a pilot and is qualified to fly just about every plane there is. She flew a drone that helped us shut down the 3D gun manufacturing business."

"This is quite the team you have, Mike; I'm rather envious."

"Let's get upstairs and see what's happening."

Irene was waiting for them.

"Great you caught the two Islamists. They're downstairs in the cells being questioned by Serious Crime officers. So far, they haven't been missed, and no alarms have been raised. They've been stripped and given prison overalls, and their clothes are being carefully examined. Now, Liz and the Reaper. The P.M.'s authority opened all the doors. Apparently, this Reaper was primed and ready to go on some mission, sitting on the runway when Liz arrived. She just said, this will do nicely and commandeered it. A lot of squabbling, you can't do that, etc., but Liz called the P.M., and he told them to give her whatever she wanted."

"It's been fitted with additional external fuel tanks, giving it significant loiter time and a range of over 1,100 miles. It has a wide range of sensors with multi-mode communications and provides video streams. That's what these technicians are doing so we can see what's going on. It is also armed with eight laser-guided missiles and 114 air-to-ground Hellfire missiles."

She smiled and said, "So if there's anyone you don't like."

"Liz is in the air right now, heading for the Mediterranean to get eyes on that Russian freighter, so as soon as these boys get things set up, we will be able to see everything that is going on. I'm going back to the messages now."

"She had the name of the freighter transferring the crate of drones from the cargo ship. 'Desert Hawk' had just sent it to the captain of the cargo ship, but no co-ordinates or transfer times. It was called the 'Herring Gull', A small coastal freighter with its home port registered as Oban in Argyll. She gave the harbour master a phone call to get more information on the freighter, only to be told he'd never heard of it. She said Oban was registered as its home port. He told her that meant nothing. It was probably a ghost ship registered in Oban for convenience and to fool the authorities, but it probably had a rendezvous with deep sea vessels at night to transfer illegal cargo. Some of these ships throw the cargo overboard tied to buoys that will inflate at a prearranged time and surface for these ghost ships to pick up; others stop and physically transfer the cargo, so I'm sorry, I've never heard of the 'Herring Gull'."

"Well, that answers a lot of questions," thought Irene.

The technicians had finished setting up the video link with the Reaper, and it was live. Irene could see ships far below and started talking to Liz, "What height are you flying at?"

"Currently 30,000 feet, but it can fly at 50,000 feet."

"The M.V. Spartan 1V is either about to leave the med or has just left and is heading for St. Petersburg. It comes in at 7,500 tons and is capable of carrying a load of 8,600 tons."

"The lens changed, and it was now in close-up mode. She could see figures on the deck of one ship. The lens changed again, and she could see the mouth of the med as it went into the Atlantic with several ships going left or right."

"Ok, I think I've got it."

The lens changed to focus on one ship.

Liz explained that it was the only ship with its A.I.S. switched off, and it was heading in the right direction. She was going to change the Reaper's flight path to reveal the stern, and that would confirm if it was the M.V. Spartan 1V or not. The screen had been set up in Irene's office, which seemed the logical place to put it. She went into the meeting room and told everyone Liz had located the ship, and it was on the screen if anyone wanted to look at it. As one, they all moved into her office.

As the Reaper moved, it highlighted the length of the ship and all the containers stacked on the deck. These containers held hundreds of Iranian Shahed - 136 Drones destined to destroy Ukraine as well as the one to be offloaded mid-Atlantic. The picture finally settled on the stern, and it verified that the ship was, in fact, the M.V. Spartan 1V.

Relief all around. Liz would be able to follow it on its path to St. Petersburg and, with the video surveillance, monitor any offloading at sea.

Irene was disturbed that she couldn't get any more information on the small coastal freighter, the "Herring Gull". It was obviously active in clandestine activities, and if "Desert Hawk" had been able to hire it for the offload at sea, so could she - into the dark web again. It didn't take her long to find it. Advertised as a coastal freighter for the discrete movement of goods, she sent a message to book their services and ask for more information. They replied almost immediately, what did she need? A pick up from an ocean-going cargo ship at the Straits of Gibraltar and delivery to the Mull of Kintyre in the next two weeks. They came back; it's possible. We're in that vicinity around that time. Can you give us dates? She replied that it depends on the movement of my ship; I can't control that. I'll enquire and get back to you as soon as possible. She signed off, thinking we could kill two birds with one stone here.

She went into the meeting room with a smile on her face that got everyone's attention, "I've been able to contact the coastal freighter that is going to unload the drones from the M.V. Spartan 1V. I told them I needed a pickup from a ship in the Straits of Gibraltar and transport to the Mull of Kintyre in the next two weeks. They told me they're in that area around that time and could possibly help. I've to get back to them when I know my dates."

The D.G. was still at the station, not wanting to leave as events unfolded, saying he hadn't experienced such excitement in years, helping to prevent a major terrorist attack and making a real contribution with the contacts he had.

"Well done, Irene," he said.

"I was thinking that because it is a ghost ship operating clandestinely and has for years, we could catch it in the act, get the Royal Navy involved, and somehow arrest the Russian ship."

"Not possible if it is in international waters. The only thing we could do is follow the freighter until it is in U.K. waters."

"OK, let's all think about it. We've got a day to maybe come up with something else. Mike, have your people been able to get anything out of Joe Banks?"

"He's not talking."

"Can I have a go?"

"By all means, I'll make the arrangements. Do you have something on him?"

"Maybe, worth a shot."

As they drove up to the High-Class Security, Irene asked Trevor if they were both armed, indicating the driver. He was somewhat surprised at the question.

"Yes, we're both armed. Do you know something we don't?"

"Possibly, our former Defence Secretary spent years working in Iran, is a fluent Arabic speaker, and kept that to himself. He's not talking, probably scared to, and just before we left, I was checking him out on the 'Dark Web' again and there was more activity in certain circles surrounding his whereabouts. For the first time, my name was mentioned, so someone is feeding information to the wrong people. It was also suggested that I should not see the light of day, and it was signed 'Desert Hawk'. He's the one in charge of bringing in the Iranian drones to attack the House of Commons. Have you been made aware of all this?"

"No, we were just told to give you close protection."

"I can't believe the stupidity of people in charge. They ask you to put your lives on the line and don't tell you why.

This is deadly serious. Iranian drones are being smuggled into the U.K. to attack our government and, at the same time, wipe out the Ukrainian Embassy here in London."

They looked at each other, and the driver muttered, "Jesus!"

"When we get back, I'll have a word with the top man, and by that, I mean the P.M. and get this sorted out. So, I would not be surprised that because my name has been mentioned, there is a leak, and there could be an attack, so be extra vigilant, boys."

"Are you not concerned?"

"Not when I've got you two protecting me."

They smiled at that, more alert but also more relaxed now that they knew what was going on.

They drove up to the front door, and this time, once the car was parked, both Trevor and the driver got out and walked either side of Irene into the prison.

Joe Banks was cuffed to a chair and waiting for her. There were only two of them in the room.

"Well Jamaal, you sure have put yourself in quite a mess." He became instantly alert and sat straight up in his chair.

"You've been quite clever but not nearly as smart as you should have been. So why did you do what you did?"

"Who the hell are you?"

"I'm the person who worked out who you really are. Now I know more about you. Shall I tell you, or do you want to reveal all?"

He was silently looking warily at her.

"Your birth mother is Iranian. You grew up in a small village in the desert with your younger brother, and your favourite bird is a hawk, a desert hawk. Your village is full of rabid jihadists, so you grew up in that environment, but you had one thing going for you: you were exceptionally clever. Iran didn't have the foresight then, but one man did, a very wealthy man and an avowed jihadist, one Osama Bin Laden, who was constantly visiting all the small villages looking for recruits. He took you under his wing, gave you a formal education, made sure you spoke English like it was your first language, and, with his money, arranged for you to have a U.K. birth certificate. You were named Joe Banks, and you were to be Osama's silent little sleeper. Only he got himself killed for his atrocities."

"So, what do you think, Jamaal? How am I doing so far? You're starting to look a bit pale. Ready to make a deal? Will I go on? The man in charge of smuggling the Iranian drones into the country using the code name 'Desert Hawk' was, of course, your little brother. Not hard to figure that out, was it?"

"Right now, you are wondering how I know all this, right? Your vanity tripped you up. Your downfall was entering a list of your favourite books on your first major political promotion. An obscure magazine that listed rising stars and their achievements, you stupidly listed working for Saudi Arabia and Iran, helping to normalise relations between the two countries. Now, why I'm here. We've been struggling to work out who 'Desert Hawk' is, and I suddenly thought if your vanity tripped you up once, you just can't help yourself, and you'd do it again, and you did. You sent a message to your little brother, in fact, several messages telling him of your achievements working for Osama Bin Laden and what to do to get these Iranian drones to the U.K. Your little brother is not quite the full shilling, is he? He kept all your messages on his server and all your instructions, and he proudly uses his code and password as 'Desert Hawk', not the brightest thing to do. So, I have literally figured it out about one hour ago. Now, do you want to make a deal?"

"As you English say, 'go to hell!'"

"Inshallah."

"Right, we're finished here."

As she left his cell, she told the guard to make sure a copy of the interview was sent immediately to the Director General of the N.C.A. and gave him the name of the police station he was at.

Irene had a sort of premonition and told Trevor and her driver to draw their weapons and be prepared for an attack as they went to the car. Nothing happened until they reached an intersection a short distance from the High-Security Prison. As they waited for the lights to change, two powerful Range Rovers slammed into them, one on the driver's side and the other on the passenger's side. The doors were blocked, and Trevor and the driver, although slightly injured and dazed, were trapped inside the car. Irene was in the back as usual and could see their method was to make sure her bodyguards were immobilized. She could get out through the rear doors, though, and could see there were two men in each car. They wore balaclavas and left their cars with Glock 19s in their hands, racing towards her. She got out one side and ran straight at them. Before they had time to react, she had jabbed both in the throat one after the other. As they fell to the ground, trying to breathe, she leaped over the bonnet of her car and jumped on top of the other two terrorists as they tried to figure out what was happening. The first one got a punch to the head that poleaxed him, and down he went.

The other raised his gun to fire, but Irene moved swiftly in close, grabbed his gun hand, and twisted it up with one hand while punching him in the solar plexus with the other. He howled once before hitting the pavement out for the count.

Trevor and the driver were stuck inside but could see everything that was going on.

"Did you see that, exclaimed the driver before he reached for the radio to call for assistance, and we're supposed to be protecting her."

It didn't take long for news of the ambush to reach the police station. The four terrorists were in the hospital being checked over. The doctors doubted if one of them would ever speak properly again and all the others could be released to a prison cell. Trevor and the driver were checked over and released. Mike offered to give them a week's leave to get over the attack, but they both vehemently wanted to stay as Irene's bodyguard and driver.

"She's created quite an impression on them as well," he thought to himself.

When Irene tried to slip into the office unnoticed, the desk sergeant called Mike and told him she was on the way. He immediately dropped everything and went to meet her. There was pure relief on his face that she was okay, and they went into the meeting room, where everyone was waiting to see her. The D.G. shook her warmly by the hand and said, "We are all so glad that you are alright and well done. I got a copy of your interview with Joe Banks, and we have all been going over it, but you should have told us before you left."

"I literally discovered it just before I left and wanted to keep it to myself until I verified it in person. Plus, someone somewhere along the line was leaking information, and I didn't want him forewarned that I was coming. It's best to see his immediate reaction."

The Superintendent and the Chief of Police were next to come in enquiring about Irene. She said she was fine but very concerned that the jihadists who attacked her knew she was going to prison. "How did they know that when I had just asked to interview Joe Banks and then literally got into a car to drive there? There is a serious leak. Is it a result of money, in the way of bribes, beliefs, empathy with a cause, or a deep-rooted spy? You may never find out when you look at how Joe Banks fooled everyone for years. We do, however, have the four jihadists who attacked me in the cells below us, so hopefully, we'll get some answers from them."

"Our next plan is to find the whereabouts of the Desert Hawk. We now know his name is Mohammed, and he is Joe Bank's brother. Another step in the right direction. We'll update you as we go along."

Mike, Fred, and the D.G. were right there as Irene spoke. When they were alone, Mike suggested a specialist be called in to interview the four men or move them to a military prison where they have different methods of extracting information from prisoners. That caused the D.G. to raise his eyebrows and Mike to comment. We are in an uncivilised war here.

11.

M.V. SPARTAN 1V

Irene had gone into her office to check in with Liz. From the monitor, she could see the ship was still in sight.

"Any problems?"

"No, it's steering a steady course."

"How long can you stay up there, Liz?"

"I've probably got another ten hours left before I need refuelling."

"OK, can you return now? I need to have a one-to-one, and you can refuel at the same time. Will you lose track of the ship by returning?"

"No, its projected course is locked into the navigation system. Turning now, see you when you get here."

Irene went into the meeting room and told everyone that the drone was returning for refuelling and that she was going to the airfield to have a heads-up with the pilot.

As she left the building, Trevor was right beside her. It was the driver this time who raised an eyebrow, and Irene said the military airfield, the one they fly all the drones from. As they drove, she brought them up to date and told them the "Desert Hawk" was none other than Joe Bank's brother Mohammed, and they would probably be taking a trip to the Islamic Students Association after they left the airfield.

When they eventually arrived at the airfield, they could see the Reaper was just landing. Trevor commented, "It's much bigger than I thought."

"They are going to refuel it, ready to take to the skies again once I talk to the pilot. You can have a closer look if you want; I'll just clear it."

She went over to the officer in charge, who looked at Trevor and the driver and motioned them over.

"I'll come and find you," Irene said and went into the flight control to speak to Liz.

They hugged each other, and Irene could see the strain on Liz's face, "How are you holding up?"

"Pretty good, actually. Once we found the ship, it's an easy matter to circle at height and keep it in sight with the technical capabilities the Reaper has at its disposal."

"Liz, we have some very serious issues to discuss before you take that drone back up in the air, and this is the most important part; it's only between the two of us. No one else, top secret, okay?"

"You have me really intrigued now. Let's have it."

"Right, you see that ship we're following, the M.V. Spartan 1V. It's a Russian cargo ship heading from Iran to St. Petersburg with hundreds of Shahed - 136 drones, each capable of carrying 36 kg of explosives. They are destined to be launched by Russia against Ukraine. I suggested to the P.M. that once the container of ten drones is offloaded mid-Atlantic to be used against the U.K., Ukraine, with its newfound marine drones, could sink it. He wasn't overly enthused with the idea, so I started thinking there'd never be another chance like this again. It would be morally wrong to allow these drones to inflict further death and destruction on Ukraine. While we have the tools to prevent that ship from ever reaching its home port."

"Funny you say that. The thought had crossed my mind as well."

"Liz, you have no idea how relieved I am to hear you say that."

"I don't understand how other countries can sit and do nothing to stop Putin from continuing with his war against Ukraine. To allow him to do what he wants, raining death and destruction on an innocent country to me is cowardly, and to use the excuse that if they get involved, Russia will use their nuclear weapons is overused as an excuse not to get involved. It's the easy way out. So, Irene Wright, my friend, we think the same."

"Great, we have to get a plan in place because I can see this coming to a head pretty soon. We have to do this so no suspicion falls on us or the U.K. government. This has been going over and over in my mind; what do you think of this? When the coastal freighter the 'Herring Gull' rendezvous with the Spartan 1V, we let the transfer take place, allow it to get far enough away from the Russians, and then get the S.B.S. to ambush it. Give them a warning shot using one of the Hellfire missiles, and use that as a cover to fire one of the laser-guided missiles at the Spartan 1V?"

"No, that wouldn't work, timings have to be precise, and there are too many what-ifs. Let the S.B.S. take care of the coastal freighter; we have to figure out a way to use one of the missiles that's not detected. It can't come from the air that would be easily spotted by too many countries. It has to come from the sea. I could program it to skim the ocean, but that brings the possibility of another ship getting in the way if it's a long run. There's a lot to work out, Irene, let's think about it and communicate by phone only. Ok, I'll give you a phone number that's not traceable or recorded."

"You can do that?"

"You'd be surprised; maybe someday, over a log fire deep in the wilderness, we can have a long chat. In the meantime, here's that number; reveal it to no one."

A buzzer went off on her console. Liz looked at it and said, "Times up, the Reaper is refuelled, and they are rolling it out on the runway now."

"Ok, between the two of us, we'll work it out, be in touch."

Irene went downstairs and joined the boys as they watched the Reaper take to the air. Trevor said, "To be able to fly that from a room just looking at instruments is something else."

"Have you looked at the pictures it sends back? The monitor is in my office back at the station?"

"No, I'd like to though."

"You are both welcome after all; you are both part of this operation, and the bonus is that the pilot is one of our detectives. A girl named Liz."

They both stopped at that, "No way," said Trevor.

"Girls fly too, you know," replied Irene.

"No, I didn't mean that just that this operation is like nothing I've ever been involved in before. You seem to get the Prime Minister's attention; you can get an advanced drone just by asking, and I must say you can certainly take care of yourself. You could probably teach me a thing or two."

"Trevor, I have a black belt, fifth Dan in karate, and I teach classes in self-defence. If you ever want to join one, you are more than welcome, and that includes you, Roger indicating her driver. It was the Prime Minister who insisted I have protection. Sometimes, it's easier just to go with the flow."

"You know, I'm going to take you up on that. Me too chimed in Roger."

"Ok, we'll start after this operation is over."

"Now we have to pay a visit to the 'Islamic Students Association'. I just want to drive slowly past and get the feel of it. They're the ones who are going to get the Iranian drones to attack the House of Commons and the Ukrainian Embassy, and the ringleader is the brother of the former Secretary of Defence whom we visited in prison the other day. Someone told them we were coming and set up that attack. We're on the verge of a breakthrough, and I just want to check it out."

As they drove past, there were a few people milling around, but not the masses she was expecting and satisfied they went back to the police station. Mike had nothing new to report. They were still interviewing the two people they had picked up outside the Ukrainian Embassy, but they were saying nothing. The only thing they had found was a half-torn piece of notepaper with some hieroglyphics in the girl's jacket pocket.

"OK, I'd like to take a look at that. Are they in the country legally? Do we know that?"

"They are not saying a word."

"So, is the next step the Home Office and deportation? Do we have a list of who is in the Islamic Students Association? Presumably, there is accommodation in that building. I'd like a copy of who is registered if we have one."

A detective brought Irene the piece of notepaper from the evidence room. She looked at it and saw that it was Arabic writing; Mike's people should have known that. She'd have to tell him about it. She took a picture of it and went into the dark web. There were people in there who could tell her what it meant. It didn't take long to get an answer; it said, "Send coordinates for the Ukrainian embassy". She was instantly raging and went out to find Mike.

He was in his office on the phone, and she just went storming in and started pacing up and down. He put the phone down immediately, "What's up?"

"You have some incompetent detectives in here. That piece of paper found in the girl's jacket was put down as scribbled hieroglyphics and dismissed as meaningless. One look at it, and I could see it was Arabic writing. Translated, it says, 'Send coordinates for the Ukrainian embassy'. How long have we had this information? You can see the implications. Mike, we have to do better than this; we've lost some valuable time here. I'm going back to my office. I've got another lead to track down," and with that, she stormed out.

Mike was equally upset and called in the detectives who were investigating the couple. There were two of them; they were told to smarten up, use their heads, and were immediately taken off the case and transferred somewhere else. Word spread pretty quickly at what had happened, and everyone redoubled their efforts.

Liz called and said the ship had slowed down, and there was a lot of activity around the top container, and she thought it was the one going to be unloaded. She was flying at 50 thousand feet to avoid detection and was keeping a running commentary.

"Hold on, I'm going to get Mike."

She left her office, took a couple of steps at the same time as Mike looked up, and shouted at him to get into her office. He quickly rushed in, and she showed him the drone pictures with all the activity around one container.

Liz continued her narrative, "They've taken two drones out of the container and seem to be opening up compartments. They're now putting the lid back on the container and covering the drones. They've also taken out what looks like some sort of gantry."

"Thanks, Liz. Keep me informed. Mike, I'll bet that's to do with the part message found in the girl's jacket. I wonder if they needed the Ukrainian Embassy coordinates and if they are programming the drones on board the ship.

I understood that was all going to be done at Machrihanish."

"Right, maybe something has changed; I'll get everyone on it right away."

Irene thought about what they were doing on board the ship and called Liz on her mobile, "Can you talk?"

"Yes, but make it quick. I've got a tricky manoeuvre coming up."

"With things that are happening here and what you discovered, I am starting to think they are only going to offload eight drones and launch two at the Ukrainian embassy from the ship. What do you think, and can I program the direction of these two drones by radio signal? Call me when you can."

"Irene was quite excited. If it was true, their new plan was to launch two drones from the ship, that would solve a lot of problems. An email was waiting for her on the dark web from the 'Herring Gull'. Have you got dates yet? We'll be in that area in two to three days. She sent a message back; it looks good. My ship will be passing through in two days. Does that work for you? Can you unload from an ocean-going ship?"

She then went into the meeting room, "It's starting to come together. The coastal freighter Herring Gull is going to be in the area in two to three days, so that confirms a handover from the Spartan 1V."

This is my suggestion: we allow the transfer of the container containing the drones to the coastal freighter, follow it, and when it is in U.K. waters and close to the Mull of Kintyre, we board it, confiscate everything on board, and arrest the captain and crew. The only thing we have to do is ask for a branch of the services to stop and board it.

"Does everyone agree with me? OK, times a wasting, I'm going to make a couple of phone calls."

The D.G. was amazed at how quickly Irene had taken control and also how quickly everyone naturally followed her and was thankful she had decided to work for the N.C.A. He looked over at Mike and said, "At this point, I could say she's your loss and our gain, but it doesn't work like that; she benefits everyone, and we are all dead lucky to have her."

Irene, at that point, was busy sending and receiving messages with the "Herring Gull". She was trying to get them to reveal the coordinates of their hook-up with the Russian ship. Working out a possible rendezvous with her fictitious cargo ship, she gave them what she had worked out. Back came the reply that's pretty close to ours. She sent it back, wouldn't it be funny if it was the same ship, what's your name? With crossed fingers, she waited for a reply. It's a Russian ship called the Spartan 1V. No, ours is a Bulgarian called the "Naked Surprise", a strange name for a ship, but there you are, no accounting for people's tastes. She was trying to establish a rapport with, presumably, the

Captain of the Herring Gull, and it seemed to be working. If our coordinates are practically the same our ships will be on top of each other. No, that won't happen. We've just received revised instructions for a pickup in two days at midnight. I hate night transfers, your position is exposed with the lights you have to use. Well, it looks like we won't be meeting up, perhaps some other time. Good luck with your transfer, and with that she signed off.

Jubilant with her success, she went into the meeting room and told everyone, "We now know the time, date and coordinates of the ship-to-ship transfer."

"How on earth did you manage that?" Fred was slowly shaking his head.

"I'll print out a copy of the messages we exchanged. We just might need them when this all goes to court. I'll relay all of this to the S.B.S. They're the ones intercepting the 'Herring Gull'."

"Are we any closer to finding Desert Hawk? How about the four jihadists who attacked us when we left the prison? Are they Iranians or a hired mob? What about the mole who knew I was going to prison?"

"Unfortunately, we are no further forward on any of them," Mike said.

"What about the girl? Did you lean on her?"

Mike just looked at her and said, "What do you think?"

"Ok, we're getting nowhere; basically, it's a stalemate, so this is what I'm going to do. I'm going to send Desert Hawk a message, and we'll see if that moves things along."

"How do you do that, if you don't mind me asking? I know you have your own methods of finding information, and I'm really curious."

"So is everyone else, Fred, interjected Mike, but I doubt you'll ever find out. Be satisfied; she gets results."

"Sorry, everyone, I have my own methods that I have built up over the years. I use computer programs and advanced algorithms, and I'm afraid I keep them to myself. Mind you, any one of you could do the same if you study and apply yourself."

Fred said, "I apologise for being so crass, Irene; I don't know what I was thinking."

"That's okay, I understand, and I hope you understand."

They both smiled at each other, and Fred added, "Do you still want to work for me?"

She smiled and said, "What do you think? I'd better get on with it."

She went into the dark web, searched out the Desert Hawk, and started typing, "So you've put out a hit on me. Silly boy. Look what it got the idiots you sent after I visited your big brother in jail. They aren't that scared of you.

They've talked quite a bit, although I doubt if one of them will ever talk properly again. Then there is Sheila, the lovely Sheila who looks better in Western clothes. After talking to her, I think she is ready to chuck the whole Muslim thing in the bin. Now, tell me what you prefer: a cell with your brother, a different prison, or do you want to go the whole way and become a martyr? It is all happening, Mohammed; it's time to make your mind up. Desert Fox."

She printed three copies, one each for Mike, Fred and the D.G., let them digest it, wait a bit for a possible reply from the Desert Hawk, and then she would tell them what she thought they should do next. She then went and made herself a coffee at the office rest area and waited. She was going to give it ten minutes, enough to finish before going on to the next stage.

12.

THE MOLE

She was about to make a move when her phone rang. It was Liz, "Great, I was about to phone you; we know the coordinates, and the ship-to-ship transfer is taking place at midnight in two days."

"I thought you should know the ship has reduced its power and is only moving at half its normal speed; why, I don't know, there is no problem navigational-wise. By the way, what you asked me before, no problem, I can do that, you can't, we'll talk about it later."

"Ok, Liz, I think they changed the ship's speed to tie in with their revised timings. When I have more info, I'll call."

She sat back, contemplating her next move. It looks like the radical approach. Surround the Islamic Students Association, arrest everyone inside, put them in a detention centre incommunicado, and find out who is legitimately allowed in the country. When to do it, it had to be soon, very soon like right away, preferably with as many people in the building as possible. The so-called students would probably congregate for prayer, which would be the best time to act. She knew Islamists say prayers five times a day at dawn, midday, afternoon, sunset, and night. She stood up to discuss it with the group when her computer started flashing. A message was coming in on the dark web. It was from Desert Hawk.

There was a knock on the door, and a detective stood there with two mobile phones in an evidence bag, he said, "These were taken from the man and woman arrested outside the Ukrainian Embassy, and there's a note to give them to you."

"What! Has anyone else looked at them?"

"No."

"Then why in hell did it take so long to get to me!" The detective just shrugged his shoulders.

Irene went raging into the Meeting Room where Mike, Fred, the D.G. and the Chief were busy beavering away. Everyone stopped what they were doing as Irene stomped in, face red and breathing heavily. Mike, rather alarmed, said, "What's wrong?"

She waved the evidence bag with the two phones inside, "These belonged to the two jihadists you arrested outside the Ukrainian Embassy, marked for my attention. Apparently, no one else has looked at them, and I'm just getting them now! How long ago were they arrested? Doesn't anyone realise how crucial this is? We have vital evidence here and it's just lying around! We need better communication. I'm going to see what's on them right now, and by the way, I was just talking to Liz. The ship has halved its speed and I presume that's to adjust to their new plans."

She then stormed out leaving everyone perplexed and angry as well.

She decided to look at the girl's phone first and leave Desert Hawk's message for the time being. The messages were mostly in Arabic, with a few in English. She plugged it into her computer, where she had special programs built in to retrieve messages that were dumped. She also had an instant translation app covering almost every spoken language. Recently, most of the messages she sent and received were for or from Mohammed, the Desert Hawk. Crucially, there was a dumped message that included a picture of a man and a woman; it was a selfie, and she recognised the girl in the cells down below. The girl called Sheila. The following dumped message was from Mohammed; it simply said, "Dump that picture!"

Her heart skipped a beat; it was a picture of Mohammed the Desert Hawk. She quickly printed two copies, one for herself and one for the meeting room. This time, she was smiling as she ran in and shouted, "Result! We have a picture of Mohammed the Desert Hawk." She put it on the table and rushed back to her office.

Everyone in the meeting room went wild, and Mike had the picture sent to all officers. The D.G. said, "What else is she going to find?"

Irene was busy scrolling through the messages, but there was nothing else that told her anything of significance, so she picked up the man's mobile and went through the same procedure as she did with Sheila's phone. The messages were all in code, but she had a program to handle that. They told Irene that this man played a subservient role and did what he was told. He was not a decision-maker, but the more she looked, the more she realised he was too subservient, so she paid him more attention. She went as far back as she could in his deleted messages, and there it was. Instructions to Mohammed on how to program the Shahed - 136 drones. He was the main man pulling the strings, staying in the background, but there was more, and her heart started racing. The final part of his message said, "Make sure Amira is in place. Did she get the job?" Her heart was tripping her as she looked for the reply. "Oh my God, there it was. Yes, she got the job."

Irene was both elated and gutted. She was gutted that the Islamic Regime had been able to get a mole into the top level of the government and elated that she knew who it was. All of the managers in the meeting room had a secretary with them, basically to do all the donkey work. Sometimes, they were present during meetings, and Amira was one of them. She was her boss' secretary.

She sat back not quite sure how to approach it, and there were so many ramifications regardless of what she did. She shook her head and looked up at the exact same time that Mike was walking past. He looked in and knew instantly there was something wrong. He went in and, quite alarmed sat down beside her. Her eyes focused on him, and she said, "I know who the mole is."

"Good God, Irene, are you sure?"

"Positive, but there are many problems surrounding the disclosure. We should talk about it first, just the two of us right now, okay?"

"Absolutely, go ahead."

"The mole is Fred Turner's secretary Amira."

She then went on to explain how she went about it, and the answer was in the two phones of the arrested jihadists. "Now I have many problems with this. I have to think of this, OK? Is Fred part of it, or is he completely unaware? Who hired her, and who did the safety checks for working at this level? Personally, I don't think Fred knows anything about it, but we have to ask. Next, everything is at a crucial point right now; we have all the pieces of the jigsaw, and I don't want to put any in the wrong place. The only thing we don't know is the location of the Desert Hawk. The man you arrested is actually in charge, but I'm sure you won't get anything out of him. He's been pretty smart the way he handled it all."

"Amira must know his whereabouts, but time is not on our side. The drones are being offloaded tomorrow at midnight. We know the coordinates and the S.B.S. is ready. The ship will be in international waters, so we can't act like pirates and board it, especially as it is a Russian ship. I think they've taken out the two drones intended for the Ukrainian Embassy and plan on launching them from the ship's deck. That will be verified when the S.B.S. board the 'Herring Gull'."

"The question is, should we allow Amira to carry on? Will arresting her somehow alert Mohammed and jeopardise our plans? We have to get those drones, or am I overthinking it, or should we let the others know? We've got twenty-four hours before the transfer takes place. What do you think?"

"I think the 'Desert Hawk' is in seventh heaven right now; everything he planned, albeit under instructions from the man in the cells down below, came from his brother Jamal and taking Amira out of action won't affect what's already in motion. Liz is on top of it, and you can verify that with her right now, can't you?"

Irene glanced at the picture the Reaper was sending and started sending a message to Liz; her reply was almost instant; it seemed to have changed. "The 'Herring Gull' is approaching the 'Spartan 1V'. I'll put it on screen now."

Sure enough, the coastal freighter was coming in astern, and the Russians had stopped dead in the water. Irene could see Derricks in action on the deck. One container was being hoisted in the air, ready to be swung over the side, and the coastal freighter slowly aligned itself underneath.

Mike said, "Looks like it's happening now, so arresting Amira won't make any difference. By the way, where is she? She was with Fred when I came in here. Don't tell me they advanced their attack, and she's done a runner!"

He stood up to alert security when he saw her walking down the corridor back to the meeting room. He breathed a sigh of relief, she must have been on a rest break. Did she even know it was happening now?

"Irene, is there any way you can find out why the transfer is taking place now?"

"Hold on, I'll try."

She went into the dark web and contacted the "Herring Gull". My ship has arrived early. Apparently, she missed one port of call. "Any chance of a hook-up?" She was surprised. He answered immediately, "Not a chance; the weather has changed dramatically here; it's getting worse, and there's no way I'm doing a transfer in pitch black in a raging storm, so I advanced the pick-up, like it or lump it."

"I'd better let you go then," and she signed off.

"Well, Mike, the gods are on our side. Apparently, there's a big storm, and the coastal freighter was not prepared to do the transfer in a raging storm and in the pitch black, so they advanced the transfer. This is good for us, changes thoughts on 'What ifs'. I suggest you arrest Amira right now and confiscate her mobile; maybe I can get Mohammed's location from it."

"Right, let's go; just wait a minute until I get some uniforms in here."

Two uniformed police came walking briskly towards them; Mike had a brief word, and then the three of them went into the room. All activity stopped, and everyone looked at Mike, wondering what was going on.

"Amira, I'm arresting you for subversive activities and actively plotting an attack on the House of Commons and the Ukrainian Embassy."

There were gasps all around, and then she suddenly made a lunge for her backpack, but the officers were too quick for her and wrestled her away. She was hissing at them and muttering in Arabic as she was handcuffed and led away.

"Let me know what's in that backpack right away," Mike called after them.

Irene came into the room, took Mike aside and whispered in his ear, "Make sure she is strip searched and her clothes examined."

He looked at her, an annoyed look on his face. He should have thought of that, said, "Right," and rushed away.

Irene faced everyone in the room. There was Fred, the D.G., the Chief, the Superintendent, and two secretaries. Outside, the office was buzzing at what was going on.

"Right, so much has happened in the last half hour. The most important search was to find out who the mole was. The answer came from the two mobile phones that belonged to the two jihadists arrested outside the Ukrainian Embassy. We got the Desert Hawk's picture from the woman's phone and discovered who the mole was from the man's phone. It was Amira, your secretary, Fred. A load of questions and investigations will follow with that discovery. We also found out that the man making out to be one of the rabble was actually the boss telling everyone what to do, including Mohammed, the Desert Hawk."

Next, the discovery that the House of Commons and the Ukrainian Embassy are targets for Iranian drones being smuggled into the country. Literally, ten minutes ago, we found out that the drones are being transferred from a Russian ship right now. Luckily, we have a drone following all of this, and the S.B.S. is waiting to intercept the 'Herring Gull' coastal freighter as soon as it enters U.K. waters.

We still have to find the 'Desert Hawk' name of Mohammed, brother of Jamal, also known as Joe Banks, our former Secretary of Defence, awaiting trial in a high-security prison. Maybe we'll get some information with the arrest of Amira.

"I know you have a lot of questions, but we haven't finished investigating yet. We're almost there, but we have to make sure the drones on that coastal freighter are immobilised."

Fred looked at her, "I'm actually gobsmacked. I'm sure everyone joins me in saying that we'd never be where we are without your hard work. Thank you so very much."

"It's not over yet, Fred. We've still got a way to go."

Just then, Mike came striding in, a triumphant look on his face, "She had a memory stick taped to her stomach. That's not all, she had a nasty-looking knife in her backpack and bundles of cash totalling eight hundred and fifty pounds."

"Did you get her phone?"

"Yes, it was also in her backpack. I know you can do something with it, so here you are."

"Good now, before I tackle them, has anyone kept the Prime Minister updated on what is happening?"

"Yes, Irene, I have," said the D.G.

"I've also told him what a magnificent job you are doing; well done."

"Thank you. Now, I first have to talk to Liz and find out what's happening on the ocean wave."

She went into her office and looked at the monitor. The "Herring Gull" was alongside the Spartan 1V, being tossed all over the place and trying to get the container safely on the deck. Irene stuck her head out of her office and shouted, "You might want to see this." Everyone piled into her office, not just those directly working on the case. The Derrick was slowly lowering the container, swinging wildly around to an equally wildly swinging deck. Someone was on the deck speaking into what looked like a mobile phone, presumably to the Derrick operator. Two men with grappling hooks were standing by on the deck.

Fred said to no one in particular, "Do you think they'll do it? The man steering that boat is brilliant. Why it hasn't crashed into the side of the cargo ship, I don't know."

The container briefly kissed the deck, and then it was off again. Another try, and the men with the grappling hooks were able to grab it and hold on. The Derrick operator quickly lowered the container again; it looked to be about a foot away, and he suddenly released it. The container hit the deck and remained intact, and the two men with the grappling hooks quickly had ropes around it and secured to stanchions on either side of the boat. The "Herring Gull" then pulled away, and they could see the Russians were on their way again by the froth coming from its stern. A tarpaulin was pulled over the container, and at first glance, no one would ever know it covered a deathly system of mass destruction.

Someone said, "Regardless of who they are and what they are doing, that was some feat of seamanship."

Everyone left her office, and Irene phoned Liz, "That was a bit hairy. Where is the ship now?"

"Still in the Atlantic off the coast of Portugal heading for the Bay of Biscay."

"Are the two drones on the deck?"

"Yes, but no one is working on them. It's pretty choppy down there."

"Any thoughts?"

"I would put my money on them going through the English Channel and into the North Sea, probably closer to Denmark, before they release them. An easy direct flight to London."

"Can you still program them?"

"Already done, my friend."

"They think all they have to do is put them on the gantry and launch them. They had already programmed them with coordinates they had received. It was the first thing they did when they received them. I've reprogrammed them to explode as soon as the button is pressed to launch."

"How can you do that? I thought you had to manually program them."

"That's the normal battlefield procedure because targets vary depending on location. These drones have a very simple computer processor made in the U.S.A. In fact, 77% of the parts Iran uses to build their Shahed - 136 Drones are U.S. made, and with the equipment I have at hand, no problem."

"Any second thoughts? Not one, you? Ditto."

"By the way, if needed, I can also signal to do the deed."

"OK, we still have to find the 'Desert Hawk', and by the way, we found out the mole is my boss' secretary Amira, who is also Iranian. Let me know if anything changes with the ship; bye for now."

Irene then sent a message to the S.B.S. Commander: "The drones have been transferred to the 'Herring Gull' and are on the way to Machrihanish. When you intercept, please let me know how many drones are on board. Thanks, Irene."

"Now, down to finding Mohammed," she said to herself. "Which do I look at first, her phone or the memory stick?" The curiosity about the memory stick and what it might contain drew her to insert it into her laptop. It was in Arabic, just as she thought, and she used her translation program to decipher it, but it was all in code. Luckily, she had developed algorithms to decode the messages on the other two jihadist phones, and as they used the same coding system, it didn't take too long to get the information.

"Wow, the D.G. is going to love this." It was a list of instructions on what universities to target, the sequence and how to vary the attacks verbal as well as physical and not just schools of learning but planned official civic events in cities across the U.K. Crucially, there was also a list of safe houses to be used in each city. This was really important information. No wonder Amira had it taped to a safe place on her body. Unfortunately, there was nothing mentioned about Mohammed and his possible whereabouts. Irene looked up, saw the D.G. was in the meeting room with Fred and Mike and printed out three copies.

She walked into the meeting room with a big smile, "You are going to love this."

All work stopped, and she had their full attention.

"That memory stick held all the planned attacks, both verbal and physical on all places of learning and cities across the U.K. as well as their safe houses."

She gave copies of their plans to each one of them. The D.G. said, "There is this old adage - to be forewarned is to be forearmed. You are a little miracle worker, Irene; well done. This is going to make such a difference."

"Ok, that was the memory stick. Now for the mobile phone; then I'll check in with Liz and the S.B.S."

She called Liz, "How are things going?"

"They are just about to enter the English Channel, and traffic is heavy, so they have slowed down considerably, and there is no activity around the two drones."

"I'm going to get in touch with the S.B.S. Commander and see what's happening there; talk to you later."

She then sent a message to the S.B.S. - "Have you got the 'Herring Gull' in sight? What are the weather conditions, and when do you plan on boarding her?"

Right, the mobile phone is next. Irene plugged it into her laptop and opened it up. As expected, all were in Arabic, but ordinary messages were not in code. It took time to read through each message, trying to find a clue as to Mohammed's whereabouts.

No luck so far. She continued searching and then went into deleted messages. That's where all the coded messages were dumped. She suddenly said, "Damn!" She had completely forgotten the "Desert Hawk" had sent her a message. There was so much going on... she went into the dark web and opened it up.

He had addressed it to the Desert Fox, "Soon, you are going to feel the full force of our movement. You won't be so flippant then!"

She decided not to reply, and soon he would be the one getting the shock of his life. If only she could locate him, he'd get an even bigger shock.

A message was coming through from the S.B.S. Boat commander, "It's pretty wild out here, forecast to abate in the next hour or so. The 'Herring Gull' is in sight, heading for land. Do you want me to intercept it now or wait until it docks? I would estimate that would be in another three or four hours."

Irene thought for a minute and said, "Better all-around if you do it as she docks and give me a shout when you're about to act. Thanks."

She went back to the meeting room, "Fred, you went to Machrihanish and checked the available accommodation. Someone has to be there to help unload and set up the drones. The coastal freighter is going to land the drones in about three to four hours. Have we got people there to make arrests?"

"Yes, given the nature of what we are facing, we have two groups of Special Forces in the area. They know the accommodation units that have been rented, and armed police are investigating the renter's backgrounds to see who might be jihadists or supporters."

"Good, because the drones are going to land in about three to four hours. Do you know if they have fingered anyone?"

"No, I don't, but I'll get in touch with those in command to let them know and find out if there are any suspects."

"Ok, I'm going back to Amira's phone to see what I can find."

She was going through the deleted messages but finding nothing, then sat back for a moment and thought, *I'm missing something*. The man arrested outside the Ukrainian Embassy along with the woman were incommunicado. We now know the man was in charge of the operation, but Amira was still operating and sending information after his arrest, so she must be getting instructions from someone else. She started going through the messages again. Nothing. She walked around a bit to clear her head, then went back to her desk, sat down and stared at the messages again. Then it hit her. There were a large number of messages coming from the same source all enquiring about her health and specific illnesses that changed focus with each e-mail. That's it, that's the anomaly. She went back to the date she went to the prison to speak to Joe Banks, and there was an email to a friend saying that her hospital appointment had been confirmed and gave the date she went to the prison. Other messages mentioned different illnesses, so prearranged illnesses had different meanings. "Very clever," she thought. However, anyone looking at these messages would think this is a chronically ill person, and she had missed it the first time around.

13.

ISLAMIC STUDENTS ASSOCIATION

She now had the e-mail address of the person in the next tier of authority, back to her old friend, the dark web. The address, after several diversions, revealed a street address for one Peter Knight. Obviously not his real name, but he was the conduit to the "Desert Hawk".

Quite excited she went into the meeting room. They all looked up, and Mike smiled and said, "You've got something, haven't you?"

"I do, and it's an address that will either lead to the whereabouts of the "Desert Hawk" or is his address."

She then went on to explain how she was able to find it. "I must say they have been very clever," said the D.G.

"You've come through once again," Mike said, "I'll organise a raid on that house and put surveillance on it right away."

The surveillance unit was an old family car with a young couple talking animatedly to each other. They watched as three men with hoodies pulled tightly over their heads walked quickly into the house. They had already observed two women dressed in Western clothes go in about fifteen minutes earlier. All of this was relayed to Mike, who was in the command car along with Fred Turner, leading several police vans full of armed officers.

Everyone had been briefed, and Mike said into his radio, "Ok! It's a go! Go, go, go."

No sirens were used, just blue lights and four vans screeched to a halt outside the house. Armed police streamed out, and half of them ran around to the back, the rest deployed around the front completely surrounding it. Mike was armed and in charge. He followed an officer wielding a battering ram who basically smashed in the front door. Fred was outside working as an observer.

Mike yelled, "Armed Police, put your hands in the air!" The other police rushed in behind him, shouting the same instructions. Half rushed up the stairs, and the rest flooded the downstairs area. Suddenly, there was a shot from upstairs, followed quickly by two more.

Mike was downstairs when the shots were fired, muttered, "Shit!" And made his way up the crowded staircase.

When he reached the top, one of his officers was clutching his chest, face grimaced in pain, and two of the jihadists were flat on the floor groaning and holding their chests. Both were covered in blood but still alive.

"What happened?"

One of the police officers said, "We reached the top shouting armed police put your hands up, this one indicating the man on the floor to the left already had a gun in his hand and when Jim reached the top, he shot him in the chest. Luckily, he had his vest on, and he's hurting right now. He'll have a bruise, but he's okay. I was right behind Jim and returned fire. Unfortunately for him, he wasn't wearing a bulletproof vest. The other one pulled a gun out of his clothes and pointed it at me, so I pulled the trigger again in self-defence. They're both alive but need a hospital."

Mike shouted, "Handcuff them all, and a thorough search, women included, and get them to the cells, tell the desk sergeant, Strip Search and inspect their clothes. You two, indicating two officers take Jim to the hospital and wait with him."

"Right boys, search the house, let's see what we've got. Be careful. Mohammed wasn't in that lot, but he could be hiding, especially in the basement; look for hidden recesses and check cupboards and wardrobes."

There were eight men and two women in the house, including the two wounded, and Mike was directing the search on the ground floor when there was a lot of shouting from the basement. He rushed to the top of the stairs leading down and saw three of his men wrestling a bearded man to the ground. One of them said, "We found this one in a hidden room at the far corner."

Mike pulled out the picture of Mohammed and looked at it then the man his men had handcuffed and pulled to his feet. The man had a bushy black beard; in the picture, the man was clean-shaven. The two were compared, and a smile crossed Mike's face and he said, "Clever Mohammed but not clever enough. Let's get him upstairs."

The top of the stairs led into the kitchen, where Mike told his men to give him a full search. Fred came and looked quizzically at Mike.

Our long-lost friend, "The Desert Hawk."

"No shit!" It was involuntary and just came out. Fred was amazed. He somehow never expected them to catch him.

Mike turned to another police officer and said, "You and your partner take another two officers and get this man to the cells, usual procedure, single cell, solitary confinement, no visitors, and an armed guard inside and outside his cell. Book him in as 'The Desert Hawk'."

"I'll be back as soon as I give this place the once over."

He looked at Fred and said, "But first." He phoned Irene. When she answered, he simply said, "We got him. He's on his way to the cells; see you shortly."

Mike and Fred started examining the house, and it was cursory as they knew the experts were on the way. There were several computers, and the hidden room in the basement held a treasure trove of electronic equipment, half of which neither Mike nor Fred knew anything about.

"Right Fred, let's get back to the office and start to analyse all of this."

When they reached the office, the atmosphere was completely different. There was a relaxed, almost jovial feeling in the air. Everyone seemed to think that because the Desert Hawk had been captured, the pressure was off. Mike knew there was still a lot to do, and it was far from being over.

There were cheers as they came into the office. Irene came over with a big smile and said well done. Mike looked at her and said it was all down to you. Well done.

Time to talk to Liz

"Where's the ship now, Liz?"

"She's almost through the Channel heading for the North Sea."

"The good news is that we have caught Mohammed, the 'Desert Hawk' just an hour ago, and I'm about to have a word with him to see if he has someone in reserve to give the order to launch the two drones at the Ukrainian Embassy. I'll be checking with the S.B.S. after this to see if they have captured the 'Herring Gull'. It's almost over; how are you holding up?"

"Doing just fine; funny thing, with this little exercise, I've been able to keep on top of my flying skills, which is most gratifying."

"Good, talk to you shortly."

She then sent a message to the S.B.S. Commander,

"What's happening? We've just arrested the so-called 'Desert Hawk', the man in charge of this attack. I need you to verify how many drones are on board… thanks, Irene."

There wasn't the same frenzied activity in the Meeting room as Irene walked in, "How is the police officer who got shot doing Mike?"

"He'll be fine. He had a big bruise on his chest. Thank God for that Kevlar vest he was wearing. The two jihadists who got shot aren't doing so well, though; touch and go with them."

"I've just talked to Liz, and the ship is almost through the English channel. I've sent a message to the S.B.S. Commander for an update, and right now, I want to have a little chat with the man of the hour. Will that be all right with you, Mike?"

"I want to see this, of course; it's all right, I'm coming with you. Right now, I presume." He stood up and the two of them walked downstairs to the cells.

The Herring Gull was doing a runner. The storm had abated, visibility had improved, and the crew had noted they were being followed for the last hour. They were close to docking, and they saw that the boat behind them had a peculiar design. The captain had not avoided being caught at sea for no reason and he was instantly alert and took out his high-powered binoculars. It had not deviated its course and was very narrow, not very wide and seemed to be quite long. At first, he thought it might be smugglers because the coast guard's boats were quite distinctive and the shape of this boat was quite different from anything he had ever seen. It was obvious they were on the same course, and he couldn't see a reason for the two of them to be heading for the same dock at the same time on this lonely stretch of Scottish coastline.

He had always followed the rule, "Better safe than sorry". When he started this line of work, he had installed a very fast and powerful engine, streamlined the exterior with the result that his boat could outrun anything the Coast Guard had. It had paid off time and time again, and he decided it was going to pay off again. He slowly powered up and changed direction to move further up the coast, where there were many inlets and small islands that he could use to evade the ship if it was trying to catch him.

The commander of the S.B.S. Unit shadowing the "Herring Gull" realised the change in the weather had allowed his quarry to see he was being followed. He had been spotted, which accounted for the increased speed and change of direction. He was surprised at the speed the coastal freighter was able to reach and could readily understand how he had never been caught. Well, he's in for a bit of a shock as he increased speed.

His boat was a new breed to the S.B.S. A V.S.V. Otherwise known as a "Very Slender Vessel" - a Halmatic V.S.V 16. It had two 750 hp engines capable of pushing it to speeds of over 60 knots. It was designed to pierce the waves rather than ride them, and that gave it an increased speed. It also had a sophisticated navigation and communication system as well as two 50-calibre machine guns. All in all, it was quite a formidable vessel.

It cut through the water like a hot knife going through butter, and as he rapidly closed in on the freighter, he was once again exhilarated at its performance. He was alongside in minutes, and everyone on the "Herring Gull" knew the game was up and slowed right down. The commander put one of his men aboard and ordered them to return to their original destination, the dock at Machrihanish.

In the meantime, the Special Forces on land had surrounded the two-holiday homes rented by the Islamic Students Association next to the now-renamed Campbeltown Airport. One unit had surrendered without a problem. There were four people inside, two men and two women, and they had several boxes of electronic gadgetry set up in the front living room. They were not so lucky with the second unit. When they were ordered to come out with their hands in the air, several shots were fired through the front window. That was the completely wrong move. Special Forces did not want a running gun battle in a holiday park area and shot several gas canisters into the house. It didn't take long for the front door to slam open and two women ran out, hands in the air screaming and coughing their guts out. They fired another canister of gas into the living room and waited. More shouted instructions to come out with their hands in the air. The reply was several more gunshots. The order was given and Special Forces went in the back door wearing gas masks. There were shouts and the sound of more shots than the all-clear was shouted. The two men had made a last stand in the kitchen. They had become martyrs and had entered their promised paradise.

Searching the house revealed more weapons and boxes with electronic gadgetry. Three helicopters were waiting at the airport; two had brought in the Special Forces, who now boarded them and flew out. They didn't want to hang about after an operation and after consultations with the armed police officers, left it to them to "tidy up", as they put it. The six remaining jihadists, two men and four women, were handcuffed and flown down to London to be interrogated along with the others already under lock and key.

The "Herring Gull" had docked alongside the V.S.V. and all crew were now being searched, handcuffed and taken away for interrogation by specialist officers in Glasgow. The Coast Guard was called to inspect and impound the Coastal Freighter. The container transferred from "Spartan 1V" was lowered to the ground and opened. There were eight drones inside. The Commander sent a message to Irene detailing what had happened.

Irene received the message as she and Mike were on their way to the cells. That gives us some leverage, she said to Mike. Just a minute, I'll let the D.G. know we've got the drones; he can breathe easier now and let the Prime Minister know. She didn't say anything about the two missing drones from the container. The less said, the better.

They kept the armed guard in the cells, just in case he was needed. The Desert Hawk was in handcuffs, hands behind his back, in his own cell, a defiant look on his face.

He looked up as Irene and Mike came in, muttered something they didn't catch and stared at them with pure hatred. Irene said, "Well, Mohammed, you do like a game of hide and seek, don't you? That's a rhetorical question by the way. Do you miss all your chats with Amira? That's not rhetorical by the way. Is she your girlfriend? Or do you just tell the women in your life what to do? Did you learn that from Osama or under the direction of your brother?"

"Who the hell are you?"

"I'm the person, the woman, who found you; just call me Desert Fox." His eyes widened, "But you're a woman!"

"Most people notice that right away, Mohammed."

"So, tell me, whose brilliant idea was it to launch a drone attack on the House of Commons? And the Ukrainian Embassy? Was that an afterthought?"

"You're not talking. Do you know that Amira is in a cell not far from your own? Faced with a very lengthy prison sentence, she's telling us all kinds of interesting things, like your deal with Russia. They wanted to hurt Ukraine. You wanted to hurt the U.K., so what better than making a deal with each other? Russia would ship the drones from Iran, who were very willing to help out and as you probably already know, supply them with drones for their invasion of Ukraine, just as long as you used two of them to attack the Ukrainian Embassy in London. How am I doing so far?"

"Mohammed, you're not saying too much. Oh, I forgot to tell you, I'm going to visit your brother later on; tell him the 'Desert Hawk' is now a guest of His Majesty's Government, just like himself. Do you want me to pass on a message?"

She had succeeded in goading him; his face was getting redder, and as he worked himself up, spittle was starting to dribble out the corner of his mouth.

"You have no idea what we are about to unleash on your unholy, decadent country. Think you are smart? Soon, the wrath of God the Almighty will rain down on your government and punish you for what you have done to our people."

"Are you talking about the ten drones you arranged to be offloaded from the 'Spartan 1V' and shipped to a remote part of southern Scotland on board the 'Herring Gull'? We intercepted that transfer just this morning."

The shock on his face was quite noticeable, and Irene followed that with, "Didn't expect that, did you, Mohammed? Now you have no one left to send them on their way. I'm afraid your plan has failed."

She had purposely not said anything about the two drones set to attack the Ukrainian Embassy, hoping to get information on any possible jihadist trained to remotely fire them from the Russian ship. She still didn't know if having people on the ship fire them or just set them up on a gantry had been arranged. Because Liz had interfered with the drone programming, she didn't want the button to be pressed too soon. Mike knew nothing about this, and she wanted Liz and the Reaper back on base so there could be no accusations that what was about to happen had anything to do with them.

Although visibly shocked, he was still defiant because he knew they had no knowledge that two drones were still on the Russian ship and awaiting instructions to fire when the ship was further into the North Sea.

"By the way, Mohammed, we are arranging for the Home Office to round up everyone in the Islamic Students Association and deport them. That's happening now."

She was watching him closely, and that statement made him visibly nervous. Right then, she knew someone in that Association was trained to trigger the firing of the two drones. For that, they would need radio equipment, and that was either in the building the so-called students used or had been set up off base. What if it is in the Iranian Embassy, she thought? Time to make a move.

"Well, Mohammed, got to go now; you enjoy the rest of your life. I hope you like porridge. Apparently, that's all they serve up for breakfast in high-security prisons, and by the very nature of your crimes, you'll be in solitary confinement. I hope you don't go Doolally, at least any more than you already are. Goodbye."

As they left the cells, Mike asked, "What was that all about?"

"We're not finished yet. The two drones destined for the Ukrainian Embassy were taken out of the container by the Russians and kept on board the ship. They are due to be launched from the ship by someone in the Islamic Students Alliance. Mohammed just confirmed that by his reaction when I said all the students were being rounded up and deported by the Home Office. It was either that or someone on the ship."

"When did you find out all of this?"

"Literally about ten minutes ago, just as we went into Mohammed's cell. The S.B.S. Commander sent me a message confirming the capture of the "Herring Gull" and its crew. The container transferred from the Russian ship only had eight drones in it. I suggest we storm that student building, put all the so-called students in a holding cell for deportation, and search for a transmitter."

"Right, I'd better get a move on and make some phone calls."

"OK, I'm going to get in touch with Liz for an update."

"What's happening, Liz?"

"The ship is just leaving the English Channel and entering the North Sea."

"Are the two drones still covered? Any activity around them?"

"Yes and no."

"Ok, we've found out that one of the Islamic students is going to activate them from a transmitter we think is in their building. I don't want you still in the air when that happens, just in case we somehow get accused when they go off."

"I still have all my armaments, so we can't be accused of that. I think it would be best to stay here and observe."

"My problem is that everyone will be going frantic thinking that two drones are going to drop on the Ukrainian embassy and blow it to smithereens, and I don't want to tell them that we rigged them so that will never happen. Any thoughts?"

"Let me think about it."

"Ok, Mike is getting set to storm the student building, put everyone in a holding cell, look for a transmitter and I presume to organise an evacuation of the Ukrainian embassy and surrounding buildings. It's completely unnecessary, but I can't tell him that. I'll stay put in my office; if you think of anything, give me a shout."

Mike had gone into the meeting room and explained that the two drones intended to wipe out the Ukrainian embassy were left on the Russian ship, and the jihadists intended to launch them from there. The "Desert Hawk" had just confirmed this by his reaction to the news that we had intercepted the "Herring Gull" containing the drones, and they were now in our possession. We believe the transmitter to launch the drones is in the Islamic Students Building, and I'm organising a team right now to storm the building and search for it.

"Do I have your approval to do that?"

He directed the question to his Chief of Police. "Yes, of course, Mike, go ahead with all speed." The D.G. chimed in.

"I'll inform the Home Office that these people should be interrogated and expelled; how were they ever allowed to enter the U.K. in the first place? What about the Ukrainian Embassy?"

"Irene is on top of that; she has Liz flying a drone over the ship as we speak. The two drones are on the deck and covered, with no sign of activity. The ship is just leaving the English Channel, which is a very busy shipping lane, and Irene has worked out that any launch would be made away from the sight of other ships, so they would wait until they are further into the North Sea perhaps off the coast of Finland, it could be anywhere there is little or no sea activity so we have time to raid the Student Building before any alert is put out to vacate the Ukrainian embassy."

The D.G. added, "Just so you know, I'm keeping the Prime Minister informed as we go along."

Irene had suggested that probably the best time to raid the building was during the time of prayer because Islamists would congregate then to observe the requirement of praying five times a day. Mike had arranged the raid for the afternoon which coincided with one of the times of prayer. Ten vans full of police, some armed and all in riot gear descended on the Islamic Students Association building at exactly 4.00 p.m.

The building was surrounded, and Mike led the charge through the front door. With shouts of armed police putting your hands in the air, most "students" were startled and readily complied; others tried to make a break for it. Mike was shouting to arrest, search and handcuff every one of them. Several of the police had been pre-assigned to immediately go to every room and look for a transmitter, checking everywhere: under beds, in cupboards.

It was absolute mayhem, girls screaming, men shouting, and then there was one shot from upstairs. Not again groaned Mike as he took the stairs two at a time. The building was on three levels, and the shot came from the second floor. As he reached the landing, he saw three police officers wrestling a bearded giant of a man to the floor. He went up and told the officers to leave the man and step aside; then he tasered him. That quietened him down.

"What happened?"

"As we came onto the landing, this man, indicating the bearded giant pulled a gun, but we were far enough in and close enough to rush him. I grabbed his gun and he pulled the trigger a moment later, but I had control and it was pointed at the floor; then Robbie here indicating another officer hit him across the knuckles with his baton, and it fell to the floor. There it is there."

"Well done the two of you, search him, put the cuffs on and get him in the van, he's going to get special treatment."

There were shouts of protest, but after the gun incident Mike shouted at everyone, "Don't take any crap from any of them!"

The transmitter was found in a cupboard on the third floor. One of the female students was trying to cover it with clothes and hide it on the top shelf at the very back.

"Mike was on that level when it was discovered."

"Search her, cuff her, take her down to the station, and hand her over to the Chief."

He then sent a message to Irene. "Success, we found the transmitter. A female student was trying to hide it. I've sent her to the Chief; perhaps you can interrogate her. I'll tell him to pass her over." He then sent a similar message to the Chief.

There were forty so-called students all on their way to detention centres to be held for interrogation and ultimate deportation from the U.K.

Mike then spent the rest of the day with other police officers, searching the building inch by inch. Any scrap of paper with writing on it was boxed, and each box was marked with the floor it came from. They had finished with the third floor and were leaving when one police officer tripped over a raised floorboard in the corner of the room. He shouted "Boss! Boss!" and Mike who was halfway down the stairs stopped and went back up.

The officer had pried up the floorboard, then, looking at what was there, started lifting more. Other police who were still there pitched in, and soon, practically the whole floor had been lifted. They all looked at each other. In between the joists, disposable phones lay side by side, along with two satellite communicator devices and several bags of white powder that looked suspiciously like cocaine. There were also pamphlets in English about the evils of Capitalism. This was quite a haul, especially the two satellite communicators that proved the so-called students were in communication with a higher authority outside the country who was obviously telling them what to do.

Mike looked at the bags of white powder and told two officers to take them immediately for analysis and to wait for the results. Then he ordered all the floorboards on the second and ground floor to be lifted.

Their efforts were rewarded immediately. More disposable phones, more bags of white powder and the bonus was found in a ground floor cupboard. A trapdoor led to a basement full of bundles of cash that were all shrink-wrapped and stacked neatly in the middle of the room. Mike shook his head, "Why on earth do they need that kind of money? Well, boys, any guesses how much?"

One of the officers said, "High denomination, I'd guess, at least five million pounds."

The girl who had tried to hide the transmitter had been handed over to Irene. The first thing she did was order her to be strip searched and her clothes examined. She was then handcuffed, and rather than being put in the cells, Irene had her brought to her office. That raised a few eyebrows, but she knew what she was doing. This was going to take a different approach.

The girl was in prison clothes and handcuffed from behind making it quite awkward for her. Irene told the two officers to remove the handcuffs and stand outside her office. She looked nervous, and Irene reckoned something like this had never happened to her before. "How is your English she asked?"

"Not bad," came the reply.

"What's your name?"

"Leila."

"That's a pretty name," Irene said with a smile.

"Would you like a coffee, tea, or anything else?"

"Thank you. A black coffee would be good." Irene got up, smiled and went to the door.

"Would someone bring me two black coffees, please?"

As she went back into her office, she looked at the girl and said, "You know you are in a lot of trouble, Leila; apart from the transmitter you were trying to hide, my colleague has told me that they have uncovered disposable phones, satellite communicators, vast quantities of drugs that look suspiciously like cocaine and enough cash to keep you very comfortable for the rest of your days."

There was a knock on the door, and a police officer brought in two black coffees.

They both relaxed a bit and started sipping from the mugs, eyeing each other up and down, trying to get a feel of the other. Irene looked quite serious as she looked straight into Leila's eyes, "You're only going to get one shot at this, Leila. You're either going to leave this office and go straight to a high-security prison facing a lengthy jail sentence, or you will be deported, never to return to this country again. It's a simple choice."

Let me explain to you; we know exactly what you were planning. The eight drones destined for the House of Commons are in our hands, and the two drones that you were going to launch from the Russian ship, the "Spartan 1V", are sitting on the deck waiting for your signal. Let me show you, and she turned her laptop around so Leila could see the screen. She spoke to Liz and asked her for a close-up of the drones on the deck.

Irene was watching her closely; Leila now had a look of almost resignation on her face. "So, what's it to be? Are you going to tell me what I want to know, or are you going straight to a high-security prison?"

The reply came almost instantly, "I'll tell you what you want to know."

"Good, a smart move, Leila. Now I just have to get a witness and a recorder."

She looked over at the Meeting room; there was only the D.G. inside. He'll have to do, she thought and waved him over as he walked over; wondering why, Irene asked for a tape recorder from a secretary outside her office.

The D.G. came into the office, and Irene said, "This is Leila, she is one of the Islamic Students Mike arrested in the Islamic Student Association's building an hour or so ago. She is the person who was tasked with wirelessly sending messages to the two drones on the Russian ship to hit the Ukrainian embassy. She has agreed to cooperate fully and tell us whatever we want to know in exchange for a straight deportation and a citation to never be allowed back into the U.K. I'm just waiting for a tape recorder before we start."

The D.G. looked at Leila with a look of animosity, and Irene bit her lip hoping he wasn't going to screw it up. The secretary came in with a tape recorder and set it up.

"Right, Leila, we're going to start. Please tell us your full name and where you are from."

"My name is Leila Suliman, and I'm from Saudi Arabia."

"How and who recruited you?"

"It was a jihadist cell in Riyadh. All my friends were joining; I was left out of everything, so I joined up as well. I was the only one who had a formal education, so I progressed. The others didn't. I was asked if I wanted to see the world and hand out leaflets in the U.K. or France. I could speak English but not French, so I came to the U.K."

"What did you do here?"

"I travelled to different cities and got involved in different student movements against the government."

"Who led you?"

"Mohammed and Amira."

"Were they partners?"

"They were lovers, if that's what you mean."

"How did you learn about the drone attack on the House of Commons and the Ukrainian embassy?"

"Mohammed explained it was his brother's idea, and he organised it."

"How did you get involved in the drone attack against the Ukrainian embassy, and who trained you?"

"Mohammed organised it as he said, 'Just in case'. He showed me what to do with the transmitter. It's really quite simple."

"Do you know of any other attack pending against the U.K.?"

"No, but there is one in progress against France."

"Do you mean a drone attack?"

"Yes."

"When?"

"I just know it is imminent; they were trying to coordinate it at the same time as the attack against the U.K."

Irene stood up and told the D.G. she had an important call to make; perhaps he could carry on with any questions he had and hastily left her office.

She went into the meeting room and phoned Francois at Interpol. He answered after two rings, "Irene, you've changed your mind."

"Not yet, Francois, but I have important information for you. To cut a long story short, we have just foiled a very complicated attack on the House of Commons and the Ukrainian embassy using drones supplied by Iran. It was a jihadist movement that initiated it."

"We have them all, and would you believe it was our Secretary of Defence who hid his true identity of being a jihadist? Anyway, one of the jihadists is cooperating and just told us a similar operation is about to take place in France."

"Mon Dieu!"

"Francois, I suggest you get over here as fast as you can or send someone from your office here or the French Embassy to question her."

"Thanks, Irene. Someone will be there within the hour."

"She only speaks English and Arabic."

"Ok, thanks."

Irene went back to her office and asked the D.G. if there was anything more or if he was satisfied. He said he was satisfied with what he had learned and he would now report to the P.M. As he left, he turned his head to Leila and said, thank you for your cooperation.

Irene told Leila she would have to stay in the cells for a couple more days, and someone from the French Embassy would be coming to talk to her about the intended drone attack on France. She nodded her head and said, "Ok."

Next, she called Liz.

"How are you holding up? There has been so much happening here it's going to take days to tell you about everything. Where is the ship just now?"

"It's in the North Sea off the coast of Norway, heading for the Baltic."

"Mike raided the so-called Islamic Student Association Building, and he found the transmitter to launch the two drones from the Russian ship and the jihadist who was in charge of it. I've had a talk with her, we've made a deal, and she's helping us. Blast, I just thought of this; I never thought to ask her what time it was scheduled to launch and how she got the coordinates. We also discovered their movement is going to also launch a drone attack against France. They wanted to do that at the same time, so it's imminent. Someone from the French embassy is coming within the hour to question the jihadist."

"I'd better go and find out about the launch times. I'll be back as fast as I can."

Mike was back, so she stuck her head in the room and told him she forgot to ask Leila when was the scheduled launch time for the drones. Did he want to come with her? He thought about it and said, *yes, maybe that's a good idea.* They went together to the cells, and as they passed Mohammed's cell, they saw that the armed guard was gone. They looked at each other, eyebrows raised, and immediately turned around and walked briskly back to the desk sergeant.

"Why was the armed guard removed from Mohammed's cell? The order came down. He was to return to normal duties."

"Was that written or verbal?"

"Written, give me a sec. I'll find it."

Mike said to Irene, "What's going on here? I've got a funny feeling about this. When the sergeant returned holding a piece of paper," Mike said, "What about the female jihadist?"

"Yes, the armed guard was also pulled from her."

"Right, I want the armed guards returned immediately and this cell put on high alert. It's quite possible that either an attempt to release them or kill them is about to be made. Go on, press the alarm!"

He called the chief, explained to him what was happening and asked him to arrange for the two jihadists to be removed to a high-security prison as soon as possible, under armed guard. Then he looked at the authorisation to remove the armed guards. It was signed by Inspector Wilson from the Armed Response Unit.

Mike said, "There is no Inspector Wilson, be on guard. We've been infiltrated!"

Another quick call to the Chief explaining and suggesting extra security at the entrance to the station and a closer inspection of everyone entering and leaving with armed guards at the entrance. The guards were to take a no-nonsense approach and be prepared for an impending attack, and there should be at least four armed police and a special forces unit given the importance and seriousness of the prisoner's crimes. A special forces unit should also accompany the prisoners to the high-security prison. The Chief said,

"You don't think that's a bit over the top, Mike?"

"Look at what happened to Irene when she went to visit the former Defence Secretary; she was ambushed, followed by a gunfight!"

"Right enough, I'll look after it right away."

"Ok, Irene, let's see Leila."

She was in the cell, sitting on a corner of the bunk, and her demeanour changed completely. "How are you, Leila?" Irene asked.

"I was fine; we had made our deal until I saw the armed guard being removed. I knew that wasn't right."

"Are you concerned at all that there might be some form of retribution against you?"

"I am now, and the sooner you honour our agreement, and I get out of this country, the happier I will be."

"One other thing I forgot to ask you. When were you supposed to launch the drones, and when did you receive the coordinates for the Ukrainian Embassy?"

"There was no specific time; I was to wait until I got a signal from the Russian ship when shipping traffic was light and before it entered the Baltic Sea. I worked out the coordinates myself using the pretext of protesting against the Ukrainian embassy as cover."

"Thanks, Leila. We were also concerned about your safety when your guard was pulled, and you will be with us until you are interviewed by the French authorities either here or in a high-security prison. If you have anything else to say, just tell the guard you want to speak to me."

When they got back to her office, there was a message. Someone from the French embassy was here to see her.

"Can someone escort him to my office, please?"

A few minutes later, he knocked on the door. It was Alfonso.

"Nice to see you again; sorry I have to be rude. There is so much going on right now. We are expecting a possible attack because of the two jihadists in the cells below. We've had several indications that it is a distinct possibility. No offence, Alfonso, but we have this imminent drone attack about to take place. Here, let me show you."

She turned her laptop around and showed him the Russian ship loaded with containers full of Iranian drones. "We have a pilot flying a Reaper above it, so we know what's happening.

The female jihadist who was going to launch two of the drones at the Ukrainian embassy told us her group was about to launch a drone attack on France.

Her name is Leila, she's been very cooperative, and we promised her freedom if she told us what we wanted to know.

She knows you're on the way to interview her; after that, she can go but cannot ever return to the U.K. Right, let's go down to the cells, and I'll introduce you. There was a group of armed police on the floor getting instructions from Mike, and she asked if one could accompany the two of them to interrogate Leila. Of course, away you go, and he waved hello to Alfonso.

When they got to the cells, Irene told the policeman to stay outside Leila's cell, be alert, and don't move an inch even if someone tells you, regardless of rank. She introduced Alfonso to Leila to keep it all civil and let her know that if she told him everything he wanted to know, things would go well for her. She told Alfonso to ring her or see her if he had a problem. Then she went back to her office."

Her phone started ringing, and she could see it was Liz. "We've got a problem; look at this."

She was right; it was a big problem. The deck of the Spartan 1V was a beehive of activity. Containers were being opened, and drones assembled.

"How long has this been going on?"

"The last fifteen minutes."

"I wonder if there is someone else, we didn't round up who is taking command now. Look at the message sent to the cells to remove the armed guard from a non-existent Inspector. It would appear that with a shipload of drones, someone is preparing to try again. They already have the coordinates for the Ukrainian embassy and the House of Commons. I'm going down to speak to Leila again; it should be ten to fifteen minutes."

Alfonso was in deep conversation with Leila when Irene returned. They were both surprised to see her again.

"Sorry, I have to interrupt. Leila, is there anyone in your organisation who would take over from you or any superior who was not in the building when we raided it? Is there anyone who would take over from Mohammed if he became incapacitated for any reason?"

"Amira is the only one I can think of; they were thick as thieves. Mind you, she had a brother she was pretty close to; she used to tell us she was always visiting him."

"Do you happen to remember his name?"

"Yes, only because she never stopped talking about him. It was Zafir, and he had an import business. He imported furniture from the Middle East; she always used to tell us if we wanted furniture, she could arrange it with knockdown prices."

"Do you remember the name of his business?"

"Only because she was constantly talking about her clever brother. Nothing elaborate simply, 'Zafir's' Wholesale Furniture Imports'."

"Do you think he could program drones?"

"I'm sure he could; Amira was constantly talking about how clever he was."

"Thank you, Leila; I might be back."

She practically ran back to her office. "Right, Liz, we have a potential culprit. I have to explain it to Mike and get a team out there as fast as we can. What's happening on the ship?"

"It looks like they have put together ten drones so far and appear to be working on others."

"Remember we talked about reprogramming drones to have a certain reaction when they are activated?"

"Yes, I do and I know what you are going to ask me; the answer is yes, once they are set up."

"Great, at least we have a backup. I have to see Mike now; talk to you later."

Mike was busy organising a defence in the event of an attack when Irene came running up to him. He looked at her and knew something was wrong.

"Let's hear it."

"We've got a big problem, then went on to explain."

"My God! One crisis to another! And it's the same crisis!"

"We have a potential break. The jihadist girl Leila is helping us. Amira, who is a mate and Mohammed's girlfriend, is currently in the cells down below. She has a brother who is in the import business. Because she was always in his company and talking him up, I think he is the one posing as Inspector Wilson and instructing the Russians to assemble the Iranian Shahed - 136 drones on board the M.V. Spartan 1V."

"Anyone else, I'd dismiss it. Do you have an address?"

"Yes, I've looked him up, and he does have an import business. Furniture from Saudi, Egypt, Morocco, Colombia, and Mexico. Ever wonder where that cocaine and cash you found underneath the floorboards at the Islamic Students Association came from?"

His eyes opened wide, "No way!"

"It all ties in, Mike. Amira made sure she got hired as Fred's secretary; she's a rabid jihadist, she's very close to her brother, you can't tell me it doesn't run in the family. We raid his warehouse and check out his furniture for false bottoms, hollow legs, etc. Remember when you searched the Students Building, you found two or three satellite communicators? I'd check for one in Zafir's house and his office. It's quite possible he is receiving instructions from abroad."

"I'm going to organise a raid immediately using police and Special Forces. Do you want to join us? You'd be there with an armed police officer."

"Would it be all right if I brought my personal protection officer, Trevor? If he wants to come, that is."

"Okay, I'll start to get things organised."

"While you're doing that, I'd better explain to the D, G., and everyone else what is going on."

"As Mike rushed past the meeting room, he saw Fred looking around at all the activity and stopped. Shouted at him to come out, briefly explained what Irene had uncovered, and said it was dangerous. Do you want to come?"

"Wild horses couldn't keep me away, thanks, Mike."

After she had explained what was going on to everyone in the Meeting room, she rushed into her office and gave the monitor a close look as she phoned Liz.

"We're on our way to raid the warehouse where we are sure the transmitter is to launch the drones. I see there isn't as much activity around the drones; what's happening?"

"They've assembled ten drones, plus the two already here makes twelve ready to launch. You don't need a gantry to launch them. They can take off from a vertical position. Five are on the bow, and seven are on the main deck."

"They have placed them around the containers holding the other drones. I think that's pretty dangerous given the power of the rockets to lift off, but that's neither here nor there since I reprogrammed them. It should be quite spectacular if someone tries to launch them."

"You've put my mind at rest, Liz; where is the ship now?"

"Heading for the Baltic."

"Ok, I'm off. I'll give you an update as soon as possible."

14.

THE SHOWDOWN

Irene joined everyone outside as Mike separated them into different groups and told them what they had to do and if there were any questions to ask himself or Irene. Special forces had their own transport, and they drove off first followed by Mike and Irene in the lead vehicle.

Fred was sitting beside Irene and commented, "I can't believe you're working for me; it should be the other way around."

"I don't know if Mike told you, but the warehouse we're raiding is owned by your ex-secretary's brother name of Zafir. I'll be concentrating on the office and any computers we find. The most important piece of equipment we're after is a radio transmitter used to launch drones. Twelve drones have been assembled on the deck of a Russian ship just entering the Baltic Sea. Whether it was done by the Russians or a team of jihadists on board, I don't know, but those drones are destined for the U.K. and are replacing the ones we intercepted in Machrihanish. I'm pretty sure it was Amira's brother who organised the replacements."

It was a large red-bricked building and from the outside looked like it could have two or three floors. All the entrance bays were at the front with two back doors. One group of special forces drove around the back; the rest went in the front. There was a lot of shouting, then the sound of gunfire. Armed police stationed themselves outside, weapons were drawn. Several men ran through the open bays; some had weapons in their hands. Police with loudspeakers ordered them to drop their weapons and put their hands in the air. Some special forces appeared behind them, and they didn't mess about. Orders were shouted and ignored, shots were fired, and bodies fell to the ground. That had the desired effect. The remaining men dropped their weapons and put their hands in the air. The armed police cuffed them and told them to lie face down on the ground.

Irene and the team in their van then entered the warehouse. She said to Trevor, "Stick with me; we're looking for radio transmitters and computers. Presumably, they will be in an office; that's what we're looking for."

Fred had decided to stay with Irene, and the three of them went looking for an office. Trevor pointed up, and there was a staircase leading up to a glassed-in area. That looked like the offices. They looked around, everything seemed clear, and they raced up the stairs. Irene reached the door first and had her hand on the handle when Trevor yelled stop! She froze, and then Fred, who was behind her, put his hands on her shoulders and moved her away from the door. Trevor nodded at them, then, gun in hand slowly opened the door shouting, "Police!" Two shots were immediately fired from the office. Trevor slammed the door fully open and slid across the floor, shooting as he went. There was a thud as a body fell to the floor.

When Irene and Fred went into the office, Trevor was checking the man on the floor. He's still alive, but he won't be for much longer if he doesn't get medical help. Two special forces soldiers had come up the stairs and told Trevor to move away. Both were medically trained, and one started working on the man while the other called for an ambulance.

Irene said, "Thanks, Trevor."

"He smiled and said, maybe we could do a trade. You teach me karate, and I'll teach you a few tricks on how to survive."

"Deal."

A stretcher had come to remove the man on the floor. Irene said, "Will he survive?"

"If we're quick."

"I wonder if that was Zafir?"

"Right, better start looking."

As they looked, they could hear the sound of smashing furniture downstairs. There was a separate office at the end of the main office, and the door was locked. Trevor took one look and put his shoulder to it. There it was. The transmitter was taking pride of place in the middle of an ornate table, and alongside it was a satellite communicator. He was getting instructions from someone outside the country. A further search revealed two bags of white powder, probably for personal use, thought Irene. There was also a drawer full of cash, quite a lot of cash more than just used for petty cash.

She turned on the computer in the corner. It was all in Arabic, but she downloaded a program that could transfer it instantly into English. She trolled through the obvious websites and then used a memorised algorithm to dig deeper. She was instantly alert and transferred to the dark web and went searching. She had a big smile now, and she said, "I know how they're going to attack France." She got out her phone and called Francois at Interpol. As soon as he answered, she said, "I know how they are going to attack you. The drones are already there, stored in a warehouse named 'Gilbert Brothers' in Lille. Good luck, talk to you later."

"How on earth did you work that out?" Fred was astounded.

"It was all in this computer; I just had to dig a little deeper and use an algorithm I knew."

Mike came up the stairs, "Well, we hit the jackpot; we had to destroy half the furniture to get it all. I don't know the price of cocaine, but I'd guess at millions of pounds and cash, that's going to take a long time to count. I'd say we've probably broken a major drug importer."

"Have we suffered any casualties, Mike?"

"No, but several jihadists are checking out their promised paradise to see if it's all what it was cracked up to be."

"I've got to get back to the office and check in with Liz. Can you arrange transport? No problem, I'll get things sorted out here and see you back at the office."

As Irene walked into the office, she was greeted with cheers, and everyone came over to shake her hand. The D.G. came over, shook her hand, and simply said, "I'm real proud of you. Well done."

Irene was finally free and went into her office. A look at the monitor, and everything seemed quiet, with rows of Shahed 136 drones lined up on the deck. She dialled up, and Liz replied without a pause, "Been waiting for you, what's happening?"

"It's all good news. We have the transmitter. It was in a warehouse we raided literally half an hour ago. I see the drones are all lined up, ready to launch; anything else?"

"No, the people who programmed them are definitely not Russian. There were four of them, and it didn't take them long. I took a little bit longer, making sure they were all reprogrammed to react in the way we discussed when they were activated."

"Well,, it's up to us now. I suggest we don't hang around and start the countdown while you get out of there. I'd still prefer it if you were on Terra Firma when it was zero hour."

"Right, I'm on my way; there are no ships on the horizon that will be anywhere near zero hour, which will be in about forty minutes."

"Ok, I'll talk to you after you land, and we can make arrangements to meet up." She signed off, closed down her laptop and walked into the meeting room.

The atmosphere was so different now; everyone was relaxed and talking about the events. Mike's team had returned and were glad they weren't given the job of counting all the cash they discovered. The police lab had verified the bags of white powder were filled with cocaine and, after a quick look at everything hidden in the furniture, estimated it was probably one of the biggest drug hauls ever made in the U.K.

Mike walked in with the Chief of police, who told everyone to gather around and congratulated everyone for all their hard work and one of the best results they had ever had. He then singled out Irene for praise and said, "Without her knowledge and expertise, it would not have been possible." She got an enthusiastic round of applause and some wild cheering. He then went on to announce that Mike had been promoted to Chief Inspector. There was more wild cheering when he said, "To celebrate all this good news and hard work, the Police department is footing the bill for eats and drinks at the local pub this coming Saturday, and all partners are invited as well." That got the loudest cheer of them all.

Everyone was breaking into little groups, and Irene said she was going out to the airfield to check in with Liz. Roger was driving with Trevor in the passenger seat, and they were listening to the news when it was interrupted by an announcement from the Coastguard.

"There has been an unexplained explosion on board a ship in the North Sea. It was a Russian cargo vessel called the M.V. Spartan 1V on its way to Saint Petersburg. Nearby ships reported a massive explosion, and it sank almost immediately. When we have more information, we will give you an update."

Trevor said, "Isn't that the one all the drones were on?"

"Yes, it was. Someone must have tried to launch them and messed up."

Liz was waiting for her at the door looking tired but with a satisfied smile creasing her face. They hugged, and she said, I've done all the paperwork, signed out and am ready for a nice long sleep. They said nothing about the explosion at sea in front of the boys, but as Liz left for some well-deserved rest, Irene leaned in and whispered, "Mission accomplished."

The next day, everyone spent doing paperwork and tidying up loose ends. Liz came into the office late in the morning looking quite refreshed and got a rapturous welcome from everyone. The D.G. and Fred had returned to their own offices, and the newly promoted Mike, the Chief and the Superintendent were all there to welcome her back. Mike said, "You did a fantastic job shadowing that ship Liz, and from fifty thousand feet up, amazing. You are some pilot, and we're lucky to have you as a member of our team."

The Chief added, "Funny how it just blew up."

"Yes, but maybe there was some diehard jihadist trying to launch them, and he messed up."

"There's also suggestions that maybe Ukraine was able to send one of their new marine drones to intercept it. That's been denied; they say they don't have the range. I guess we'll never know."

"I don't suppose we ever will," said Irene.

The Chief's secretary came over and said, "The Prime Minister is on the phone."

He came back a few minutes later and looked at Irene, "He wants you to see him right away."

Roger and Trevor took her to Downing Street and waited for her in the lobby.

Irene was ushered into the P.M.'s office, where he immediately stood up and shook her hand warmly and asked her to have a seat on the sofa across from his desk. He sat on a side chair. There were only the two of them, and she wondered what was coming up.

He started off, "Mrs. Wright, you have no idea what you have done for this country, and it owes you a great debt of gratitude. I said this once before, and I get the feeling I'll be saying it again. If there's ever anything I can do to repay you, just ask."

Irene smiled, "Any chance of borrowing one of your planes again?"

"Of course, no problem."

"There are just two other things; first, and I want you to think very carefully about this… I would like you to come and work for me as my personal advisor."

"Second, and this is why there are only the two of us in here. How did you blow up that ship in the North Sea?"

"I don't know what you are talking about, sir," Irene replied. "And, that's why I want you to come and work for me."

The End.